A Williamson *Little Hands*® Book

Early Learning Skill-Builders

Colors, Shapes, Numbers & Letters

Mary Tomczyk

ages 2–6

Illustrations by Karen Weiss

WILLIAMSON PUBLISHING CHARLOTTE, VERMONT

Library of Congress Cataloging-in-Publication Data

Tomczyk, Mary, 1954-
Early learning skill-builders : colors, shapes, numbers & letters /Mary Tomczyk.
p. cm. -- (A Williamson Little Hands book)
Includes index.
ISBN 1-885593-84-8
1. Education, Preschool--Activity programs. 2. Readiness for school. I. Title. II. Series.

LB1140.35.C74T64 2003
372.21--dc21

2003043099

Little Hands® series editor: **Susan Williamson**
Project editor: **Vicky Congdon**
Interior design: **Dana Pierson**
Interior illustrations: **Karen Weiss**
Cover design: **Marie Ferrante-Doyle**
Cover photo: **Glen Moody Photography**
Printing: **Capital City Press**

Williamson Publishing Co.
P.O. Box 185 • Charlotte, VT 05445
(800) 234-8791

Manufactured in the United States of America

10 9 8 7 6 5 4 3

Portions of this book were previously published as *Shapes, Sizes, & More Surprises!*

Dedication

To my children Dawn, David, Jim, and Kim who brought these ideas to life.

To my husband, Fred, who has been my partner and greatest encourager — without him, this book would never have been written.

Contents

A Message to Grown-Ups

Early Childhood Skills: A Key to Learning Success

How can you, as a parent or an adult working with pre-school children, stimulate a love for learning? It's easy! Research continues to confirm that the quality of experiences young children have in the first few years of life is critical to their social, intellectual, and physical development. An enriched environment stimulates children, and provides a foundation for problem-solving, reasoning, and other higher-level thinking skills.

Preschool children exposed to enriched learning experiences are better able to develop the appropriate school-readiness skills that are one of the key factors in school success. What's more, children with a strong start tend to find school an exciting place and are on their way to becoming lifelong learners.

Fortunately, this experience-rich environment is not difficult to provide. Young children have an almost insatiable desire to explore the world around them. The seemingly simple activities that parents and other adults share with young children — the games we play, the sounds we listen for on a walk, the shapes we point out on a car ride or in a magazine, the toys we help sort at cleanup time — can provide a wealth of learning.

On the following pages, you'll find more than 50 developmentally appropriate experiences designed to be used as a guide for planning preschool and daycare curriculums as well as by parents and other adults at home. Use these hands-on activities and games to introduce and develop basic early-learning skills such as color, shape, number, and letter recognition; counting; comparing and contrasting; and sorting. In addition to practicing a specific skill, many of the activities also sharpen observation and listening skills and exercise verbal skills. All of these learning experiences are appealingly presented as "fun and games,"

providing practice in important social interactions such as taking turns and sharing.

The activities are grouped by basic early-learning skills. **Helping Hands** at the beginning of each chapter explains why that skill is important and how the activities reinforce it. **More Skill-Builders!** offers additional activities to build on the main activity for further learning challenges or to give children another approach to a particular skill. **Little Hands Story Corner**™ reinforces the crucial preliteracy connection with read-aloud recommendations.

Preschool children vary widely in their abilities, experiences, and interests, so there is no single "right age" when children learn these skills. If an activity seems too difficult or doesn't spark interest, try another one and go back to that one another time. Some activities require more of your input, some less. Young children should always be supervised, however. Be wary, of course, of children putting objects in their mouths (like the dried beans used in several activities) and decide when tools such as staplers, safety scissors, or hole punches can be used safely.

Learning is an adventure — and you are the guide! Be enthusiastic, laugh often, listen carefully, respond thoughtfully, and enjoy this journey together!

Remember that your underlying goal is to help children process and make sense of the world around them, so look for opportunities to apply what they are learning in practical ways. My sincere hope is that these activities will help each child to acquire a lifelong love of learning and inquiry.

Mary Tomczyk

A Message to Read to Children

Learning Is Fun!

Would you like to go on an exciting adventure full of fun surprises? That's what learning is — a journey to explore the world around us! Along the way, you'll discover things you already know and lots of new things as well. And if you make a few mistakes, that's part of learning, too! Best of all, when you learn something new, it's like finding a little treasure: You can keep what you've learned forever!

This book is full of fun things for you to do. There are counting games, art projects, alphabet activities, things to sort and compare, color walks, stories to tell, guessing games about animals, and lots more.

Most of the activities you can do by yourself, some will require a grown-up partner, and many of them are games to play with a friend. Remember always to ask for help if you need it: That's one important way that we learn!

Lots of wonderful experiences are waiting for you in the pages of this book. Are you ready to begin the adventure?

Shaping Up!

A ball, a box, an apple ... everything has its own special shape — even you! The shape of each thing helps us to know what it is. Let's have some fun with different shapes! Once you learn the basic shapes like a square or a circle, you'll see that shapes are all around you!

Helping

Hands

Recognizing common shapes is an excellent visual discrimination activity that develops *observation skills.* It also involves *comparing and contrasting* one object to another, so it lays the groundwork for understanding categories of objects. Shape identification develops awareness of *spatial relationships.*

Drawing or cutting out the shapes reinforces this learning and helps develop fine motor skills. Draw the shapes lightly in pencil first and let the child trace over them until she learns to form them independently.

In pattern activities, such as Pattern-of-Shapes Place Mat (pages 16 to 17), encourage children to create patterns of their own to develop more complex independent thinking skills and to build memory.

Shape Art

Which shape is your favorite: a circle, a square, a rectangle, or a triangle?

Make your favorite shape into a piece of art to hang in your room.

What you need

- ● Marker
- ■ Cereal-box cardboard
- ▲ Scissors (for grown-up use)
- ● Glue
- ■ Decorations: uncooked pasta, scraps of fabric and gift wrap, buttons, dried beans
- ▲ String

What you do

1. Draw your favorite shape on the cardboard and ask a grown-up to cut it out for you.
2. Spread the glue evenly over the cardboard shape. Press some decorations into the glue until the shape is completely covered. Let dry.
3. To hang, push string through a hole at the top of the shape, tie, and hang in a special place. Now try a different shape!

Note to adults: Small objects can present a choking hazard; please supervise toddlers closely.

Alike and Different

Close your eyes and run your fingers gently along the edges of the shape you just made. Can you tell what the shape is without peeking? Can you feel the difference between the hard pasta or beans and the soft piece of fabric?

I'm practicing...

- shape recognition and formation
- compare and contrast skills
- fine motor skills

Little Hands Story Corner™

Square, Triangle, Round, Skinny by Vladimir Radunsky
Round Is a Mooncake by Roseanne Thong

Tips for Scissors

Open, close, open, close!
Scissors are very helpful tools.

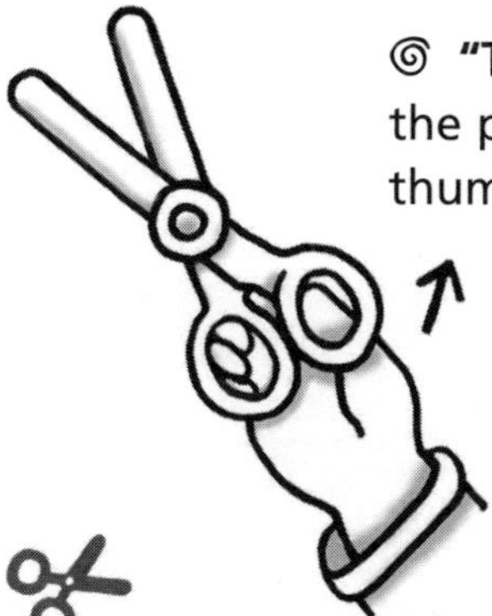

- **"Thumbs up!"** Make sure that the part of the scissors with your thumb in it is always facing up.

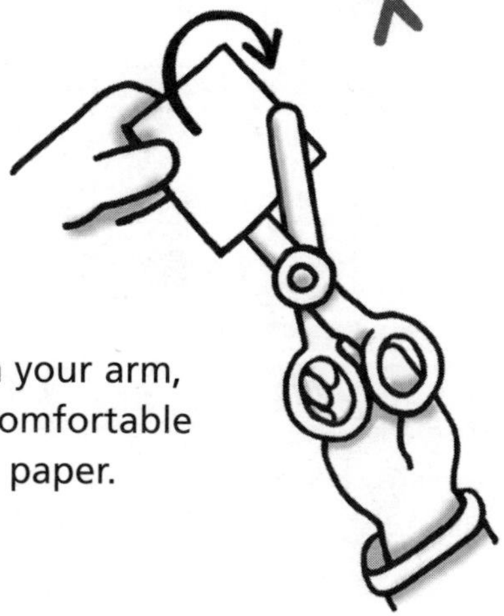

- **"Turn the paper, not the scissors!"** If you turn the scissors, you'll turn your arm, and that's not as comfortable as just turning the paper.

Picture Perfect!

You can make a frame! You'll need a large card-board shape with a center shape cut out of it (made by a grown-up). What shape is your frame? What shape is the opening in the center? Are they alike or different?

Decorate the outer edges of your picture frame with colored squares, circles, and triangles cut from construction paper or shiny pieces of gift wrap. Tape a picture to the back and hang up your frame.

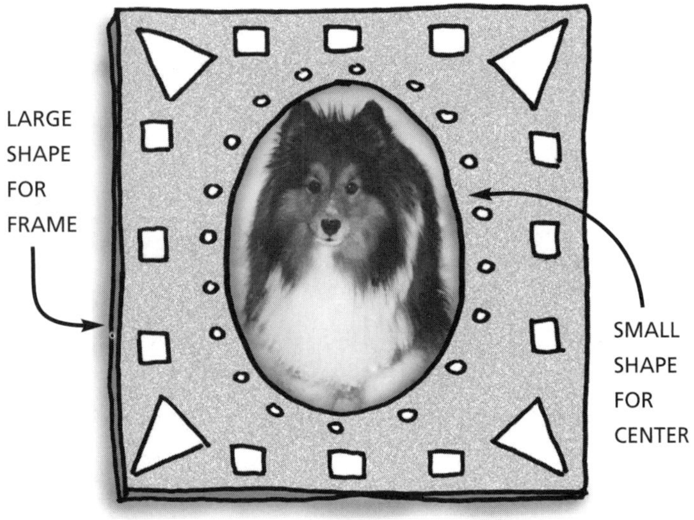

More Skill-Builders!

- **Celebrate a special shape day.** On Circle Day, you can bake muffins in round tins, eat lunch in a circle with friends, or take a walk to find five round objects.

Can you find round shapes in the picture?

My Favorite-Shapes Shirt

You can carry your favorite shapes around with you wherever you go when you wear them on the front of a T-shirt that you decorated!

What you need

- ● Old newspaper
- ■ Light-colored T-shirt
- ▲ Pencil
- ● Cardboard templates of a circle, a square, a triangle, and a rectangle (made by a grown-up)
- ■ Self-adhesive paper (like Con-Tact paper)
- ▲ Scissors (for grown-up use)
- ● Sponge
- ■ Fabric paint, on paper plate or in shallow dish

What you do

1. Cover a table with the newspaper. Lay the shirt on it.

2. Trace the shape templates onto the back of the adhesive paper. A grown-up will cut out the shapes to make *stencils*, which are shapes you can paint over.

3. Peel the backing off the stencils and stick them on the T-shirt to make a design with the shapes. Dip the sponge lightly into the paint and dab it over all the uncovered areas. (It's OK if the paint goes onto the stencil.)

4. Let the shirt dry completely before removing the stencils. See the shapes underneath?

STENCILS

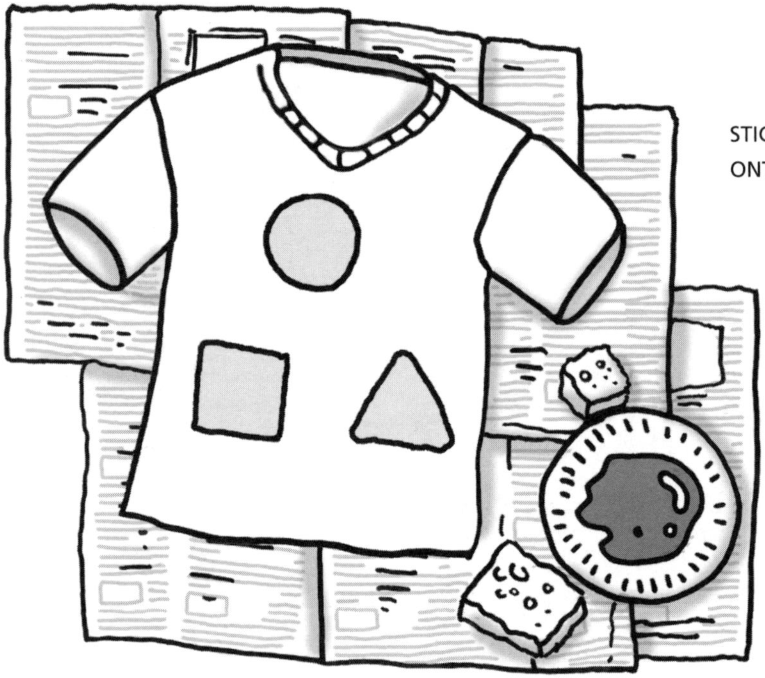

STICK CUTOUT SHAPES ONTO SHIRT FRONT

DIP SPONGE INTO PAINT AND DAB OVER SHAPES

I'm practicing...

* shape recognition and formation
* compare and contrast skills
* fine motor skills

More Skill-Builders!

- **Print with sponge shapes.** Instead of using adhesive paper to make a stencil, cut sponges into the shapes you want. Paint one side and press them onto the shirt. Press and lift straight up without smudging.

- **Make shape pictures.** You can create a pattern (page 16) such as ● ■ ● ■ ● ■ ● ■, or you can print all one shape using different colors. (Be sure to wash your sponge before dipping in a new color.)

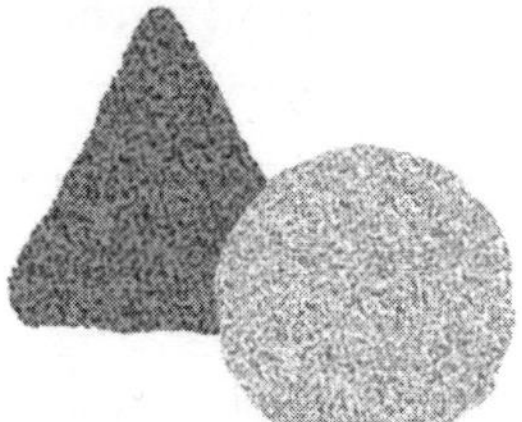

Little Hands Story Corner™

Angelina Ballerina's Shapes by Katharine Holabird

My Book of Shapes

What better place to collect and show off your favorite shape than in your very own book of shapes!

What you need

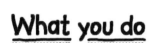

- ● Child safety scissors
- ■ Old magazines
- ▲ Glue
- ● Construction paper
- ■ Crayons
- ▲ Textured items: scraps of fabric, uncooked pasta, sandpaper, etc.
- ● Hole punch
- ■ Yarn

What you do

1. Choose your favorite shape — circle, square, triangle, or rectangle.
2. Find some magazine pictures with your special shape in them. Cut them out.
3. Glue the cut-out shapes onto several sheets of construction paper.

Note to adults: Small objects can present a choking hazard; please supervise toddlers closely.

4. To make a cover, draw a big picture of your special shape on a sheet of construction paper. Then glue pasta, sandpaper, or cotton balls onto your shape so it will be fun to touch.

5. Holding your pages together like a book, ask a grown-up to punch three holes through the left side and help you tie the pages together with the yarn. What a nice shape book you've made!

I'm practicing...

* observation skills
* shape recognition and formation
* fine motor skills
* compare and contrast skills
* categorizing

Little Hands Story Corner™

Shapes, Shapes, Shapes by Tana Hoban
What Is Round? What Is Square? by Rebecca Kai Datlich

More Skill-Builders!

- **Choose another shape to make into a book.** How many shape books would you like to have?
- **Trace over each shape with your finger** and say the name of the shape out loud as you read your book of shapes.
- **Close your eyes and touch the shape on the cover of your book.** Can you "see" the shape through your fingertips? Now, can you draw the shape in the air without looking at it?

Pattern-of-Shapes Place Mat

Can you figure out what comes next in this sentence? "Circle-circle-square. Circle-circle-square. Circle-circle ... " You're right! A square! Those shapes repeat to make a pattern.

Patterns are all around you. They can be made of shapes, colors, numbers, letters, or designs. Make a special place mat with your very own shape pattern so everyone will know where you sit.

Note to adults: To keep the place mat clean, simply preserve between two pieces of self-adhesive paper (like Con-Tact paper).

What you need

- Cardboard templates of a circle, a square, a triangle, and a rectangle (made by a grown-up)
- Pencil
- Child safety scissors
- Colored construction paper
- Glue

What you do

1. Using the cardboard templates, trace and cut out several of each shape from different colors of paper.

2. Choose any two shapes to make a simple pattern like circle-square, circle-square, circle-square.

3. Choose another color of construction paper for your place mat. Glue the shapes on, using your shape pattern.

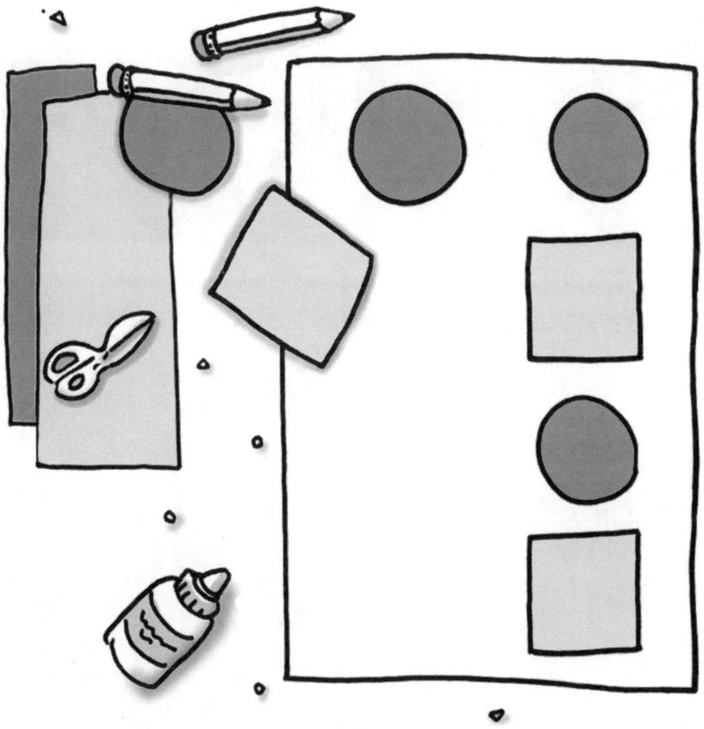

GLUE CUTOUTS ON PLACE MAT IN A PATTERN OF REPEATING COLORS OR SHAPES

More Skill-Builders!

- **Make a different place mat for each family member.** Tell why you chose certain colors and shapes for each mat.
- **Look for other patterns at the dinner table.** Take turns around the dinner table pointing out patterns in the room.

I'm practicing...

* shape recognition and formation
* pattern recognition and identification
* compare and contrast skills
* color recognition
* counting in sequence
* number concepts (quantity)
* fine motor skills

Little Hands Story Corner™

What's Next, Nina? by Sue Kassirer
Beep Beep, Vroom Vroom! by Stuart J. Murphy
Pattern Fish and *Pattern Bugs* by Trudy Harris

Be a Shape Detective

Guess what you'll be looking for when you're a shape detective? You'll be hunting for circles, squares, triangles, and rectangles — in the strangest places!

What you need

- ● Paper
- ■ Pencil or crayon

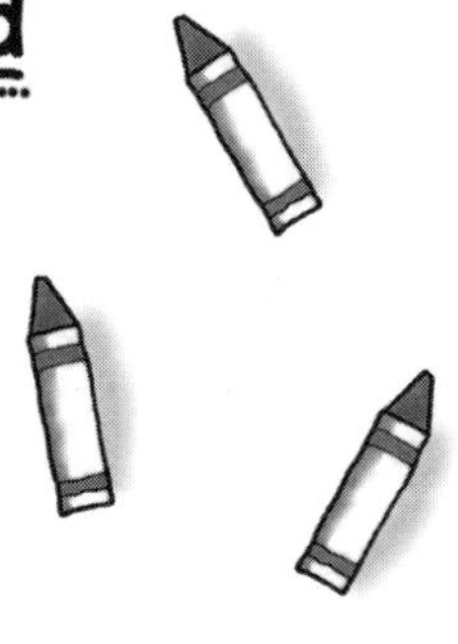

What you do

1. On the left-hand side of a sheet of paper, draw a circle, a square, a triangle, and a rectangle down the side of the paper. Carefully study each shape.

2. Now it's time to go on a shape search! Walk slowly around the room. Each time you find something that matches one of the shapes on your paper, make a check mark next to that shape. Here's a hint to start: Look carefully at the doors — can you recognize what shape they are? Now try another room.

3. Count up all your check marks. How many shapes did you find altogether? Which shape did you see the most times? Which did you find the least?

I'm practicing...

* observation skills
* shape recognition and formation
* fine motor skills
* compare and contrast skills
* counting in sequence
* number concepts (quantity)
* categorizing

Little Hands Story Corner™

The Wing on a Flea: A Book About Shapes by Ed Emberley

The Shape Detective by Angela C. Santomero

Match That Shape!

Did you know you can make a special deck of your very own shape cards? Then you can play this fun memory game with a friend!

What you need

- ● Pencil or crayon
- ■ Index cards
- ▲ A partner

What you do

1. Draw three or four simple shapes, one on each index card.

2. Have your partner hold up a card with a shape on it and then turn it facedown. Can you draw the shape without looking? (If not, take a peek.) Try the others.

3. Now you hold up shape cards for your partner to draw.

I'm practicing...

* observation skills
* shape recognition and formation
* memory skills
* counting in sequence
* number concepts (quantity)
* fine motor skills
* taking turns
* working with a partner

Little Hands Story Corner™

Color Farm and *Color Zoo* by Lois Ehlert

More Skill-Builders!

- **Play Make a Match!** Make a second set of cards. Mix all the cards together and lay them all out facedown. Take turns choosing two cards: If they match, keep them; if not, put them back. The winner is the player with the most matches.

The Shape Song

Sing this fun shape song to the tune of "Twinkle, Twinkle, Little Star"!

What you need

- ● Child safety scissors
- ■ Construction paper

What you do

1. Cut a circle, a square, and a triangle out of the paper.
2. Sit with your shapes in front of you. Listen carefully — and be ready to change shapes!

Put your circle in the air,
Hold it high and keep it there,

Put your square behind your back,
Now please hold it in your lap,

Put your triangle on your toes,
Now please hold it on your nose.

Hold your circle in your hand,
Now it's time for you to stand,

Wave your triangle at the door,
Now please put it on the floor,

Hold your square and jump,
jump, jump,
Now throw your square up, up, up!

Alike and Different

Look carefully at your paper shapes. They look very different from each other. Each has a different number of corners. Can you count the corners a triangle has? How many corners does a square have? What about a circle? It doesn't have any corners at all! But circles, squares, and triangles are alike, because all of them are shapes. What other shapes do you know? How many corners do they have?

I'm practicing...

* listening
* shape recognition and formation
* fine and gross motor skills
* language comprehension
* following sequential directions

Little Hands Story Corner™

So Many Circles, So Many Squares by Tana Hoban
When a Line Bends ... A Shape Begins by Rhonda Gowler Greene
Squarehead by Harriet Ziefert

More Skill-Builders!

- **Here is a fun little rhyme about circles.** Try it by yourself or in a circle of friends!

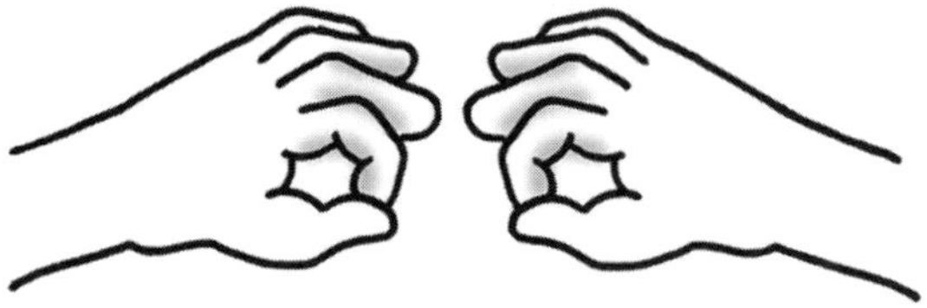

A circle big, a circle small
(make finger circles)

As round as round can be,
(hold up the circles)

Watch my two arms and you will see
(raise arms slowly)

A great big circle over me!
(connect arms overhead)

- **Let's do some thinking puzzles:** What do you play with that's the same shape as a circle? Here's a hint: It bounces and you can roll it or catch it! That's right, it's a ball!
- **Can you think of something that's shaped like a square?** If you're in your house and want to look outside, what can you look through? A window can be a square!
- **Here's one that starts out as a circle but we cut it into triangles to eat it.** It is a tasty dessert that's often made with fruit. Can you guess? A slice of pie can be a triangle!

A World of Colors

Just about everywhere you look you see color! There are lots of colors all around us — spring flowers, cars whizzing by, even your favorite shirt! Color makes our world beautiful and exciting. It's fun to play with colors, too!

Helping

Hands

These activities will help children to identify the basic colors. Once the child is comfortable recognizing and naming them, you can then use color to practice other skills such as counting and pattern recognition. Color recognition also works well in simple sorting activities that develop comparing and contrasting skills and lay the basis for categorizing. And of course playing with color is instrumental in developing visual imagery and exercising creative expression through all kinds of art and crafts activities.

Tissue-Paper Rainbow

It's exciting to catch a glimpse of a rainbow in the sky after it rains, isn't it? Here's a colorful rainbow you can make anytime, rain or shine!

What you need

- ● Pencil
- ■ White construction paper
- ▲ Various colors of tissue paper
- ● Cotton swabs
- ■ Glue in a shallow dish

What you do

1. With a grown-up's help, draw lines on the construction paper to form the bands of the rainbow. A real rainbow has seven bands of color, but yours can have fewer if you like.

2. Tear each color of tissue paper into lots of small pieces and put them in piles.

3. Dip a swab into the glue and spread it on one band of your rainbow. Press one color of tissue-paper pieces onto the glue. Then, cover the other bands of your rainbow with glue and tissue-paper pieces. Let your rainbow dry.

More Skill-Builders!

- **Make a suncatcher!** Cut shapes out of a sheet of construction paper and glue different-colored pieces of tissue paper over the holes. Hang in your bedroom window!
- **"Grow" a rainbow of flowers!** Crumple up pieces of different-colored tissue paper and glue them on paper for blossoms. Draw on stems and leaves for a colorful garden!

I'm practicing...

* color recognition
* compare and contrast skills
* categorizing
* counting in sequence
* number concepts (quantity)
* fine motor skills

Little Hands Story Corner™

Planting a Rainbow by Lois Ehlert
A Rainbow of My Own by Don Freeman
All the Colors of the Rainbow by Allan Fowler

Color Sort

This fun game will turn you into a color-sorting pro! Play by yourself or with a friend.

What you need

- ● Cardboard templates of a circle, a square, and a triangle (made by a grown-up)
- ■ Pencil or crayon
- ▲ Red, blue, and yellow construction paper
- ● Child safety scissors
- ■ Tape
- ▲ 3 coffee cans or other containers

What you do

1. Use the cardboard templates to trace two of each shape on each color of construction paper.

2. Cut out each of the shapes. When you are finished, you will have six of each shape.

3. Cut out a small piece of each color paper and tape one color on each can.

4. Mix all your shapes together. Sort all of the colored shapes into their matching-color coffee cans. Then, dump the shapes out, mix them all up, and sort them again!

I'm practicing...

* color recognition
* shape recognition
* compare and contrast skills
* sorting
* counting in sequence
* number concepts (quantity)
* fine motor skills

Little Hands Story Corner™

Is It Red? Is It Yellow? Is It Blue? by Tana Hoban
Little Blue and Little Yellow by Leo Lionni
Color Dance by Ann Jonas

More Skill-Builders!

- **Sort by shape.** Put the circles in one can, the squares in another, and the triangles in the third.
- **Use your sense of touch to sort.** Close your eyes and feel the shapes with your fingers. Can you sort them without peeking?

Color Walk

Look around you, and what do you see? Lots of wonderful colors! Let's go for a walk — indoors or out — and see what colors you can find.

What you need

- Crayons
- Paper

What you do

1. Choose one color that you would like to hunt for on a color walk. You can call it your color of the day!

2. Walk around indoors looking for things that have your color of the day. Try looking in a drawer, under a table, or in a closet to find your color.

3. Take a walk outdoors with a grown-up to look for your color of the day. Remember to look all around you: the sky, the trees, the ground, the birds … all sorts of things might have your color.

4. Draw a picture of some of the things you found. Be sure to use the crayon that is your color of the day.

I'm practicing…

* color recognition
* compare and contrast skills
* categorizing
* memory skills
* fine and gross motor skills
* observation skills

More Skill-Builders!

- **Celebrate your color of the day!** Dress in that color, eat snacks in that color, paint a picture in that color, or make a paper chain in shades of that color.
- **Sort your colors by shade.** The same color can have different *shades* — everything from dark to light and lots in-between. Can you sort the items you found on your color walk from lightest to darkest?
- **Take a survey of people's favorite colors.** Ask your family members which is their favorite color. Do any of them have the same favorite as you?

Little Hands Story Corner™

Colors Everywhere by Tana Hoban
Brown Bear, Brown Bear, What Do You See? by Bill Martin, Jr.
Hailstones and Halibut Bones: Adventures in Color by Mary O'Neill

Racing Colors

Which of these three colors do you think will win the race: red, blue, or yellow? You can race by yourself or with other kids!

What you need

- ● Crayons
- ■ White construction paper
- ▲ 3 small toy cars or 3 wooden blocks
- ● Scrap paper
- ■ Paper lunch bag

What you do

1. Ask a grown-up to help you make a game board: Draw two parallel lines down the length of the white paper. Label one end START and the other end FINISH, and draw five circles from start to finish down each lane. Color all the circles in the first lane red, the second lane yellow, and the third lane blue.

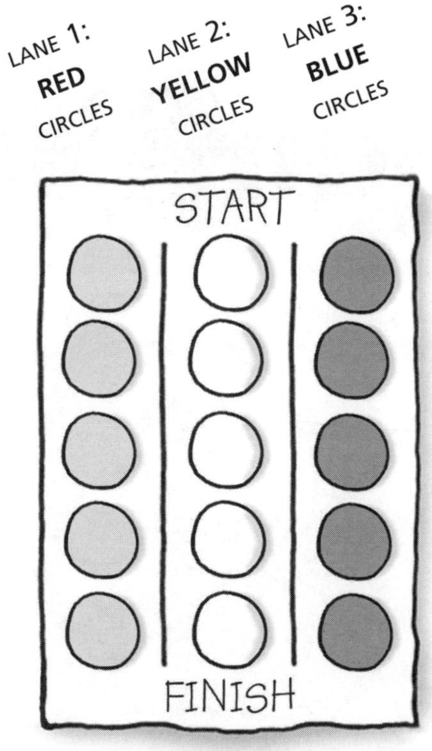

2. Tear three small pieces from the scrap paper. Color one piece red, one blue, and one yellow. Put all three slips in the bag. You're ready to play!

3. Line up the cars at START, one in each lane. Draw one slip of paper from the bag. The color on the board that matches the slip of paper tells you which car to move. Move that car one spot forward. Put the slip of paper back in the bag, shake it up, and draw again. Keep playing until one of the cars reaches FINISH. That car is the winner! Which color was it?

I'm practicing...

* color recognition
* counting in sequence
* number concepts (quantity)
* compare and contrast skills
* categorizing
* fine motor skills

Little Hands Story Corner™

Red, Blue, Yellow Shoe by Tana Hoban
My Many-Colored Day by Dr. Seuss

More Skill-Builders!

- **Invite two kids to play with you.** Each player can choose a color and take turns in order. See whose color wins the most races.

Ice-Cube Color Painting

We use ice to cool down a drink, to skate on, and to keep food cold, but did you know you can use an ice cube as a paintbrush?

What you need

- ● Popsicle sticks
- ■ Partially frozen ice cubes in the tray
- ▲ Spoon
- ● Tempera paints, on paper plates or in shallow dishes
- ■ Heavy paper

What you do

1. To make ice-cube paintbrushes, poke Popsicle sticks into the ice cubes. Let freeze solid, then ask a grown-up to help you remove them from the tray.

2. With the spoon, make some small dots of paint on the paper. Holding it by the handle, rub the paintbrush back and forth over the paint. What happens?

3. Try putting small amounts of other colors on your paper and rubbing those with another ice-cube paintbrush. What happens if you swirl two colors together? Make the most colorful painting you can! (If your paper is getting too wet, start a new painting on a fresh sheet.)

4. Let your picture dry completely. Now you have a special picture to hang in your room!

I'm practicing...

* color recognition
* using my imagination
* creative expression
* fine motor skills

Little Hands Story Corner™

Mouse Paint by Ellen Stohl Walsh
The Big Orange Splot by Daniel Pinkwater

Big Colorful Balloons

Make a big bunch of colorful balloons to show off all the colors you know!

What you need

- Red, green, blue, and yellow markers
- White construction paper
- Tempera paints that match the markers, on paper plates or in shallow dishes
- Damp paper towel

What you do

1. Draw four big balloon-shaped circles on the paper, each with a different color marker.

2. Dip a finger in one color paint and fill that colored circle with fingerprints.

3. Wipe off your finger with the paper towel and pick another color to print. Continue until you have filled each balloon with its color. With a marker, draw strings for the balloons.

More Skill-Builders!

- **Add more colors.** How about orange, or purple, or pink balloons?
- **Glue on strings.** A grown-up can cut pieces of string, one for each balloon. Glue them along the marker line so they look just like real balloons!

I'm practicing...

* color recognition
* compare and contrast skills
* categorizing
* fine motor skills

Little Hands Story Corner™

A Color of His Own by Leo Lionni
Purple, Yellow, Green by Robert Munsch
Where Do Balloons Go? by Jamie Leigh Curtis

Our Amazing Alphabet!

Thanks to the 26 letters in the alphabet, you can spell your name, write "I love you" to a special friend, or enjoy hearing a favorite story. Do you know what letter your name begins with? Here you'll learn lots more letters!

Helping Hands

Letter recognition and formation provide the foundation for learning the associated sounds that is essential for strong reading and writing skills. Start simple, working with only one or two letters at a time. Talk about how each capital letter is shaped to reinforce visual memory of it. Lightly sketch the letters first so the child can trace over them until he learns them. Matching and memory games are other fun ways to reinforce the mental image of the letter and are an excellent way to learn the entire alphabet, a few letters at a time. Then, point them out everywhere you go!

ABC Cookies

What better way to get to know the letters of the alphabet than to eat them? How do you think your name will taste?

What you need

- ● Mixing bowl
- ■ 1 cup (250 ml) vegetable shortening or $^1/_2$ cup (125 ml) margarine and $^1/_2$ cup (125 ml) vegetable shortening
- ▲ $1^1/_2$ cups (375 ml) sugar
- ● 4 eggs
- ■ 1 tablespoon (15 ml) vanilla
- ▲ 2 teaspoons (10 ml) anise flavoring (optional)
- ● 5 cups ($1^1/_4$ L) flour
- ■ 4 teaspoons (20 ml) baking powder
- ▲ Mixer
- ● Cookie sheets
- ■ Spatula
- ▲ Cooling racks

What you do

1. After washing your hands, ask a grown-up to help you measure out the shortening and the sugar into a bowl. Help mix these ingredients to a creamy consistency. Add the eggs, vanilla, and anise flavoring.

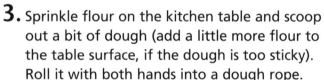

2. Add the flour and baking powder, a little at a time. A grown-up can use the mixer on low to combine these ingredients each time you add more.

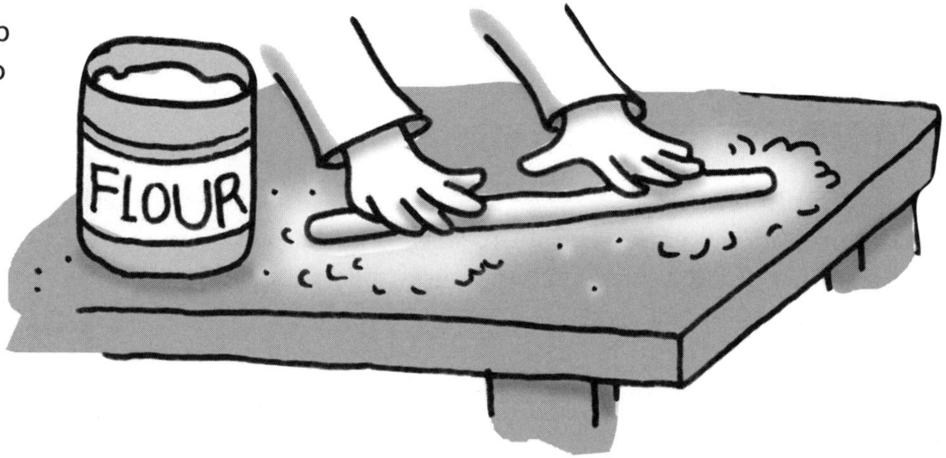

3. Sprinkle flour on the kitchen table and scoop out a bit of dough (add a little more flour to the table surface, if the dough is too sticky). Roll it with both hands into a dough rope.

4. Choose a letter of the alphabet that you'd like to learn (perhaps the first letter of your name). A grown-up can roll a dough rope and make that letter. You copy it. Now try the first letter of your last name. After you make each letter, say it aloud as you place it on the cookie sheet. You've made your initials! Practice making as many letters as you like.

5. A grown-up can bake your cookies in a 350°F (180°C) oven for 12 to 15 minutes. After they've cooled, choose your favorite letter to eat. Now you can tell your friends that you ate a letter today!

I'm practicing...

* alphabet awareness
* letter recognition and formation
* number concepts (quantity)
* following multiple-step directions
* measuring skills
* fine motor skills

More Skill-Builders!

- **Add some color to your cookies!** Separate the dough into three sections. Add a few drops of different food coloring to each. Work the color into the dough by squeezing and squashing it with your hands. What colors did you choose?
- **Spell out your whole name.** Form and bake all the letters of your name for an extra-special crunchy treat! For a birthday surprise, spell out the guest of honor's name in colorful cookie dough.

Little Hands Story Corner™

Eating the Alphabet by Lois Ehlert
ABC Yummy by Lisa Jahn Clough

Trace a Letter

Ready to try some magic writing? Your finger will be the magic pencil, and your hand will be your magic eraser. You'll write in sand instead of on paper.

What you need

- ● Pie pan or cookie sheet
- ■ Sand or salt

What you do

1. Cover the bottom of the pan or cookie sheet with sand or salt.

2. Ask a grown-up to draw a letter in the pan. Trace over it with your magic pencil (your finger) and say its name aloud.

3. To magically erase your letter, smooth the sand so it covers the bottom again. Now try drawing the letter by yourself, saying its name.

I'm practicing...

* alphabet awareness
* letter recognition and formation
* vocabulary and verbal skills
* memory skills
* fine motor skills
* sensory awareness

Little Hands Story Corner™

ABC by Dr. Seuss
ABC: What Do You See? by Arlene Alda
Chicka Chicka Boom Boom by John Archambault

More Skill-Builders!

- **Spell your name in the sand.** Use a large cookie sheet or baking pan so you have plenty of room for a whole word.

- **Name that letter!** Ask a grown-up to write letters on different pieces of paper. Put the paper in a bowl. Now you and a friend can take turns removing a piece of paper from the bowl, drawing the letter in the sand, and naming what each other drew.

- **Make sand shapes.** Trace around a yogurt container to make a circle or a milk carton to make a square. Can you make that shape without the container?

Bumpy Bean Letters

Dried beans make colorful and three-dimensional alphabet art! And touching the bumpy shape of the letter will help you remember it.

What you need

- ● Old newspaper
- ■ Construction paper
- ▲ Pencil
- ● Glue
- ■ Dried beans

Note to adults: Dried beans can present a choking hazard; please supervise toddlers closely.

What you do

1. Cover the table with the newspaper. On the construction paper, draw a letter you are learning. Or, ask a grown-up to draw a letter you would like to learn so you can copy it. For fun, draw a big shape around it, such as a **G** inside a triangle.

2. Spread glue along the letter. Place the beans on the glue, putting them as close together as you can. You just made a bean letter!

3. Outline the shape in glue. Again, glue the beans close together along the outline.

More Skill-Builders!

- **Sort your beans** into piles of light-colored and dark-colored ones. Make your letter out of one pile and your shape out of the other.
- **Close your eyes and run your fingers over your bean letter.** Does feeling it help you picture it in your mind?

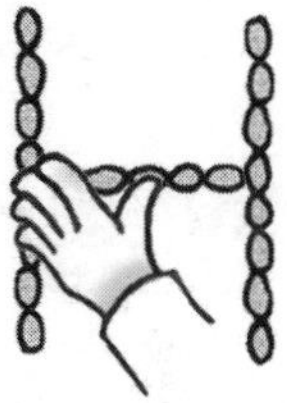

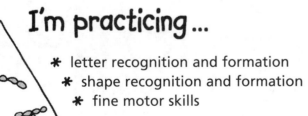

I'm practicing...

- letter recognition and formation
- shape recognition and formation
- fine motor skills

Little Hands Story Corner™

26 Letters and 99 Cents by Tana Hoban
Alphabatics by Suse MacDonald
The Straw, the Coal, and the Bean by the Brothers Grimm
Jack in the Beanstalk

The Name Game

Match up the letters to spell one of your favorite words — your name!

What you need

- Index cards
- Marker or crayon

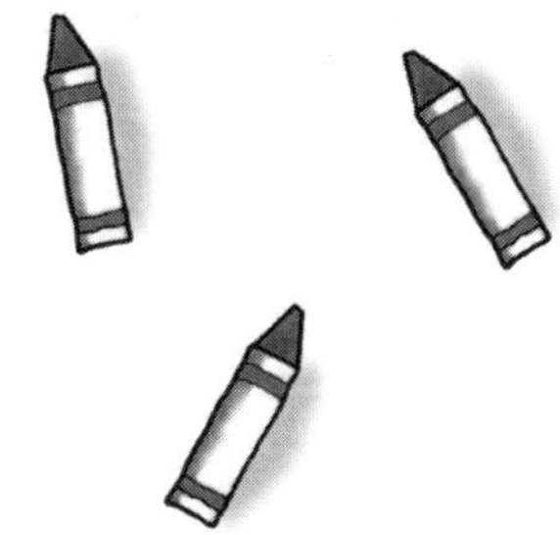

What you do

1. Draw each of the letters of your name on index cards, writing one letter on each card. Then, make a second set of letter cards.

2. Lay out the letters of your name in order. Match up the second set of letters by placing them right below each of the letters in your name. Say the name of each letter as you put down the card. You've spelled your name twice! Mix up the letters and do it again.

I'm practicing...

* letter recognition and formation
* observation skills
* name recognition and formation
* compare and contrast skills
* fine motor skills

Little Hands Story Corner™

Andy: That's My Name by Tomie dePaola

The Z Was Zapped by Chris Van Allsburg

More Skill-Builders!

- **What's missing?** Ask a grown-up to lay out the letters of your name, leaving one out. Can you name the missing one?
- **Try more names!** Try "Mom," "Dad," or the names of sisters, brothers, or pets.

- **See it and spell it.** Write the letters on a piece of paper just below the cards, naming each letter as you write it. You just wrote your name — great job!

Alphabet Cards

When you can match the letters in your name (The Name Game, pages 46 to 47), ask a grown-up to help you make two sets of cards for the whole alphabet. Now you can play lots of matching games — what a fun way to learn all 26 letters!

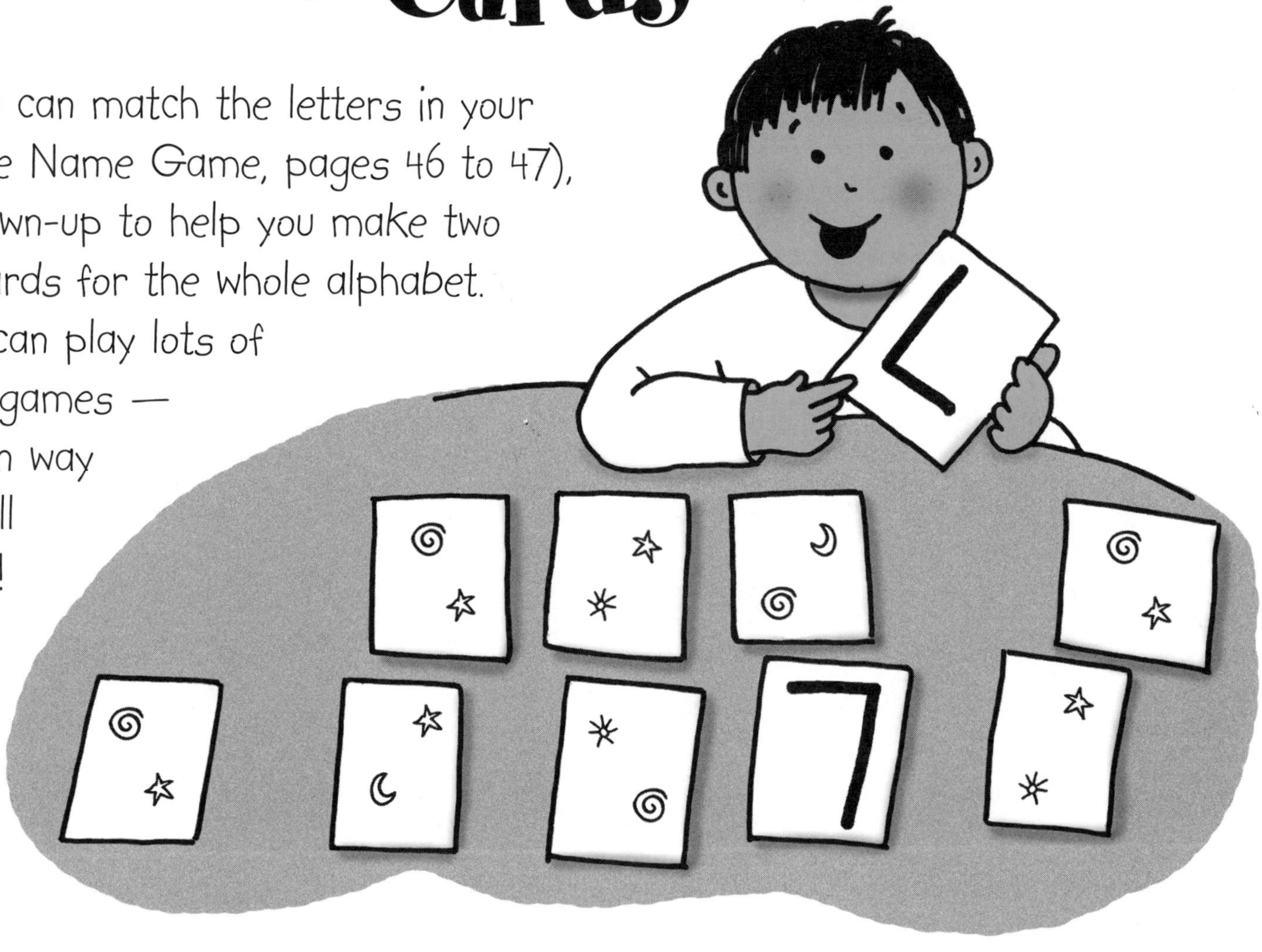

What you do

Here are some games you can play with your alphabet cards:

Memory match: Take out five pairs of matching letters. Mix them up and turn them all facedown. Turn them over, two at a time. Do they match? If so, name them and set the pair aside. If not, turn them over and try again. Play until you've matched up all the letters.

I've got a match: Take out six pairs of matching letters. Mix up one set and place it facedown in a pile. Hold the other set in your hand. A grown-up can turn over the top one in the pile, and you find the matching letter in your hand. Name the letter as you set down the pair. Continue until you have matched them all up. Add more pairs as you learn more letters.

"Fish" for a match: Take out six pairs of matching letters. Mix them up and deal all the cards to you and a partner. Take turns drawing cards from each other — when you havea pair, name it and set it down.

I'm practicing...

* alphabet awareness
* letter recognition and formation
* observation skills
* memory skills
* compare and contrast skills
* taking turns
* working with a partner
* fine motor skills

Little Hands Story Corner™

ABC Drive! by Naomi Howard

The Icky Bug Alphabet Book by Jerry Pallotta

On Market Street by Arnold Lobel

Big Body Letters

All 26 letters of the alphabet are made up of straight lines, curved lines, or a little of both. To make some alphabet shapes with your body, you can stand up straight as a pencil or bend over and curve to the floor.

What you need

- An alphabet book
- A partner (optional)

What you do

1. Find a picture of the letter L or the letter T. Those are both straight-line letters.

2. Can you make your body look like an L and then like a T? Which one could you do with a partner?

3. Now try a curved letter like a C.

4. Look at a picture of your favorite letter. Is it made up of curves, straight lines, or a combination of both? Try to make your body match the picture, or work with a partner to make the letter.

I'm practicing...

* alphabet awareness
* letter recognition and formation
* observation skills
* compare and contrast skills
* fine and gross motor skills

Sense It!

Your eyes help you to tell the difference between the letters of the alphabet. You have other senses, in addition to sight, that can help you learn: touch, taste, hearing, and smell. What sense would help you recognize a song on the radio? Which one would help tell you that cookies were baking in the oven?

More Skill-Builders!

- **Guess that letter!** Ask a partner to make her body into a letter of the alphabet. Can you tell what the letter is? Ask for a hint if you aren't sure.
- **Give them a hand!** Try using your fingers to form a letter and see if your partner can guess what it is.

- **Palm drawings.** Here's a fun game that shows another way to recognize letters — through your sense of touch! Close your eyes and have your partner softly draw a letter on your palm with his or her finger. Try to picture the letter in your mind as your feel your partner trace it. Can you guess it?

Little Hands Story Corner™

Apples, Alligators and Also Alphabets by Odette and Bruce Johnson
Alphabet City by Stephen T. Johnson
The Alphabet Tree by Leo Lionni

Count Me In!

How many fingers do you have? If you can have three cookies for dessert, how do you know when you've had your share? How many stories would you like to read? When you learn to count, you can answer all these questions — and lots more!

Helping Hands

This chapter provides fun, easy ways to learn numbers and practice counting in sequence. It introduces the idea of one-to-one correspondence, which forms the basis for understanding the concept of quantity. Other activities will help a child to associate the number symbols we use with the quantities they represent and to practice forming the numbers.

Just as with letters (pages 38 to 52), start simple, introducing a few numbers at a time until the child is comfortable with one through 10. Count along with him until he's ready to do it independently, or write the numbers lightly in pencil so the child can trace over them. Numbers can then be used to reinforce other skills in the book: draw *three* circles, find *two* blue socks, and so on.

Muffin-Cup Count

Put out as many cups as you need when you're learning to count until you can go all the way from one to 10!

What you need

- 10 paper muffin cups
- 10 small stones, dried beans, buttons, or other small objects

Note to adults: Small objects can present a choking hazard; please supervise toddlers closely.

What you do

As you count each number from one to 10 out loud, place one stone or other object in each muffin cup. Did you have just the right number of holders for the stones?

I'm practicing...

* counting in sequence
* number concepts (quantity)
* one-to-one correspondence
* fine motor skills

Little Hands Story Corner™

Turtle Splash! by Cathryn Falwell
The Crayon Counting Book by Pam Munoz Ryan

More Skill-Builders!

- **Now set two stones aside.** Put the remaining stones in the muffin cups, one per cup. Will you have too many stones, too many cups, or just the right number? If you count the number of stones now, how many will you have? Is that number more or less than the number of muffin cups?
- **A grown-up can set out a number of stones on the table.** Now you count out the same number from your pile, dropping them into the muffin cups as you count.

Count-and-Eat Necklace

This jewelry is special because you can snack on it while you're counting!

What you need

- Shoelace
- Cheerios

What you do

1. Tie a large knot at one end of the shoelace.

2. Pick up one piece of cereal at a time and string it on the shoelace (counting as you go). A grown-up can help you count as you string the pieces. When you have lots of cereal on the shoelace, ask a grown-up to tie the ends together so you can slide it loosely over your head. Your necklace is ready to wear … and to eat!

3. During the day, snack on your cereal necklace. Count how many you munch and how many are left. Are you hungry enough to eat four pieces? Six pieces? Ten pieces? How many pieces are left?

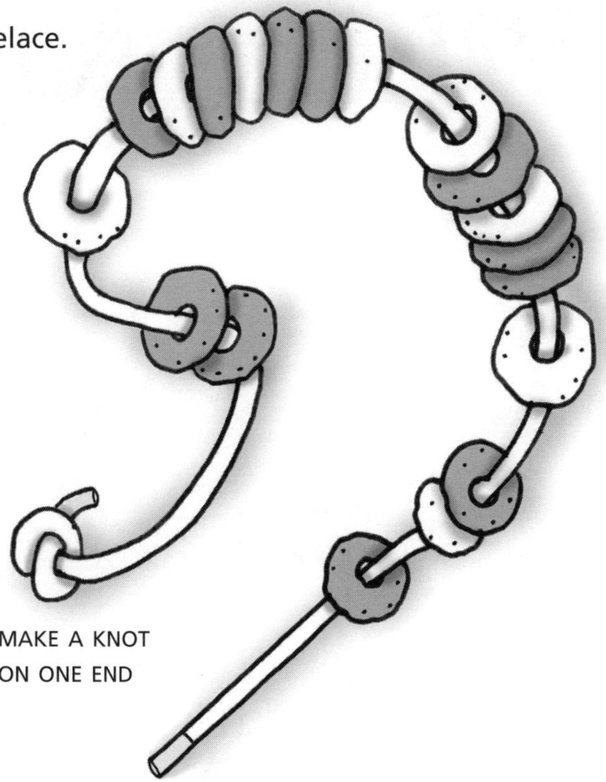

More Skill-Builders!

- **More or less?** Pour out a small dish of Cheerios or other cereal. Guess how many pieces are in the dish. Then, with the help of a grown-up, count the pieces and see how close you came with your guess. Did you think there were *more* pieces or *fewer* pieces than there really were?

I'm practicing...

* counting in sequence
* number concepts (quantity)
* one-to-one correspondence
* fine motor skills

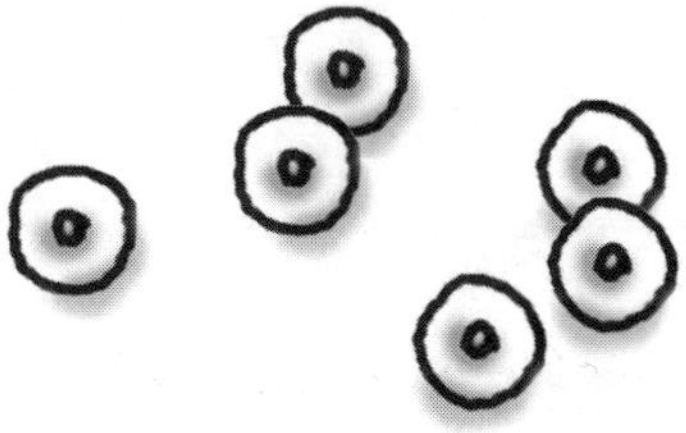

Little Hands Story Corner™

Five Creatures by Emily Jenkins
Let's Count by Tana Hoban

Jump on the Number!

Find the numbers — using your feet!

What you need

- Marker or crayon
- 10 sheets of paper
- Masking tape
- A partner (optional)

What you do

1. Write the numbers one through 10, one per sheet, so that each number fills an entire sheet of paper.

2. Tape your numbers on the floor about 2" to 3" (5 to 7.5 cm) apart in order from one to 10.

3. Jump to each number, starting with one and ending at 10, calling out each number as you land on it.

4. If you want, take turns with a partner, calling out any number from one to 10 so she can jump on it. Now your partner calls out a number for you.

I'm practicing...

* counting in sequence
* number concepts (quantity)
* number recognition and formation
* language comprehension
* fine and gross motor skills

Little Hands Story Corner™

One Fish, Two Fish, Red Fish, Blue Fish by Dr. Seuss
Anno's Counting Book by Mitsumasa Anno

More Skill-Builders!

- **Pretend that you're a bunny** and hop on both feet to the number. Or, crawl like an ant to each number. You could even pretend to be a dump truck, "beeping" as you back up to each number. What else can you pretend to be?
- **Roll and jump!** Tape an 11 and a 12 to the floor. Each time you roll the dice, count the dots and hop to that number on the floor.
- **Ask a friend to roll the dice,** count the number of dots, and call out any of the following for you to do that many times: jump, hop on one foot, run, hip wiggles, jumping jacks, toe taps, or hand claps.

Bounce and Count

Bounce it, roll it, throw it, toss it, catch it — and now, count it, too!

What you need

- ● Large ball that bounces
- ■ A partner

What you do

1. Sit on the ground facing your partner. Leave some space between the two of you. Practice rolling the ball back and forth.

2. When you are ready to play, say "One!" in a loud voice as you roll the ball to your partner. Your partner says "Two!" before rolling it back to you. You say "Three!" and send the ball back. Keep rolling the ball back and forth until you can't count any higher.

3. Now try tossing the ball, letting it bounce once before your partner catches it. Before you toss it, call out a number. When your partner catches the ball, she must say the next number. Count each time the ball is tossed and each time it is caught.

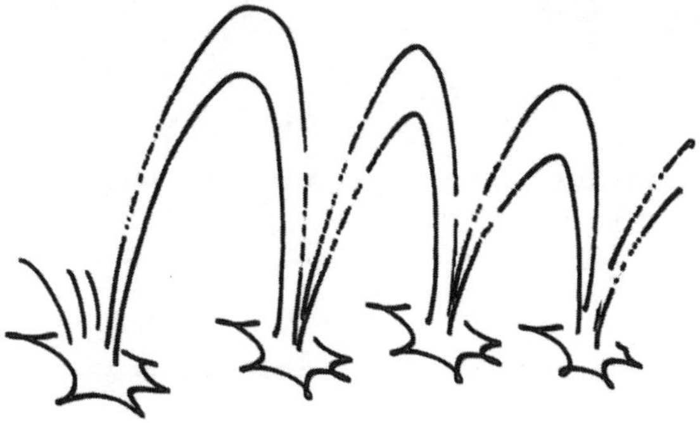

I'm practicing...

* number concepts (quantity)
* counting in sequence
* one-to-one correspondence
* listening
* vocabulary and verbal skills
* taking turns
* working with a partner
* fine and gross motor skills

- **Call out a number between one and five;** you and your partner roll the ball back and forth that many times. Now let your partner choose the next number.
- **Bounce a ball up and down without catching it in-between.** How many times in a row can you do it without missing it? Count the number of dribbles out loud.

Little Hands Story Corner™

Fish Eyes: A Book You Can Count On by Lois Ehlert
1, 2, 3 by Tana Hoban

Number Puzzles

Puzzles are always fun to do — and these are extra special because they're all about numbers!

What you need

- 5 cardboard rectangles 5" x 7" (12.5 x 17.5 cm), made by a grown-up
- Dark crayon or marker
- Textured items: bottle caps, uncooked pasta, pretzels, sandpaper, cotton balls, scraps of fabric, etc.
- Glue
- Scissors (for grown-up use)

Note to adults: Small objects can present a choking hazard; please supervise toddlers closely.

What you do

1. Draw a wiggly line down the center of each rectangle to make two puzzle pieces.

2. On the left side of each rectangle, write a number. Write 1 on the first rectangle, 2 on the second rectangle, and so on, up to 5.

3. On the right side of the 1 rectangle, glue on one textured item. On the right side of the 2 rectangle, glue on two textured objects. Continue until you have completed all the rectangles. Let dry. A grown-up can cut each rectangle apart along the wiggly line so that you end up with two puzzle pieces.

4. Mix up the puzzle pieces and try to put them together by matching the written numbers with the number of objects. To be sure you don't miss any, touch each object as you count it.

CUT APART ALONG THE WIGGLY LINE ON EACH CARD

I'm practicing...

* number concepts (quantity)
* number recognition and formation
* counting in sequence
* one-to-one correspondence
* memory skills
* fine motor skills

More Skill-Builders!

• **Put together the number puzzles with your eyes closed.** Have a partner call out a number, and you find the matching puzzle piece by counting the glued objects with your fingers.

Little Hands Story Corner™

Doggies by Sandra Boynton
Angelina Ballerina's 1, 2, 3 by Katharine Holabird

Corny Counting Cards

These 3-D cards are handy for remembering what numbers look like because you can just run your fingers over the shapes!

What you need

- Old newspaper
- 10 large index cards
- Pencil
- Glue
- Dried corn, beans, or other large seeds

Note to adults: Small objects can present a choking hazard; please supervise toddlers closely.

What you do

1. Cover the table with the newspaper. On one card, draw a number 1.

2. Spread glue along the number. Place the corn on the glue, putting the kernels as close together as you can. Now you have a corn counting card!

3. Make a set of counting cards from one to 10. Practice counting to 10, laying down each card as you say the number.

I'm practicing...

* number concepts (quantity)
* number recognition and formation
* counting in sequence
* memory skills
* fine motor skills

Little Hands Story Corner™

The Icky Bug Counting Book by Jerry Pallotta

More Skill-Builders!

- **With your eyes closed, feel each corn number with your fingers.** Can you picture the number in your mind? Keeping your eyes closed, say the number if you can.
- **Mix them up!** Can you mix up your cards and then lay them out in order from one to 10?
- **Count and Match.** Here's a game to play with a friend. You set out a number of objects, like five blocks. Your friend counts them up and places the corn card that shows the correct number next to them. Now it's your turn!

Count-and-Match Dot Designs

Counting dot designs on dice can be a fun way to learn and play with numbers and patterns! (For another pattern activity, see the Pattern-of-Shapes Place Mat, page 16.)

What you need

- 8 dice
- A partner

Note to adults: Dice can present a choking hazard; please supervise toddlers closely.

What you do

1. Roll one die. Count the number of dots that are showing. Set down another die so that the same number of dots are showing on top. Take turns with a partner.

2. Roll two dice and place two more dice showing the same numbers. Take turns with a partner.

3. Place four dice in a pattern, such as one dot, two dots, one dot, two dots. See if your partner can create the same pattern. Now it's your turn!

4. Ask your partner to roll two dice. Take a close look at the dot design. Then, ask your partner to cover the dice. Now see if you can set up your dice the same way.

I'm practicing...

* counting in sequence
* observation skills
* compare and contrast skills
* pattern recognition and identification
* visual memory skills
* fine motor skills
* working with a partner
* taking turns

Little Hands Story Corner™

Ten Black Dots by Donald Crews

Look Once, Look Twice by Janet Marshall

More Skill-Builders!

- **Toss one die until it lands with only one dot on top.** How many times did you have to toss it? Will it always take that many tosses to get one dot? Try it and see!
- **Close your eyes while a partner hides two dice in the room.** Ask your partner to clap faster as you get closer to finding the hiding place.

Count-the-Dots Creatures

Use your imagination and the roll of the dice to make these funny creatures look very unusual, indeed!

What you need

- ● Paper
- ■ Crayons
- ▲ Dice

Note to adults: Dice can present a choking hazard; please supervise toddlers closely.

What you do

1. In the center of the sheet of paper, draw a body for your creature in any shape you want — a circle, a square, a triangle, a peanut shape, or a squiggly shape.

2. Decide what you'd like to add next: arms, legs, heads, feet, tails. Roll the dice and count how many dots are showing. If you chose to draw legs, and you rolled a five, draw five legs on your creature.

3. Continue rolling the dice and adding body parts, including details like how many eyes, ears, noses, mouths, fingers, and toes your creature will have.

4. Color your creature and hang up your picture.

ROLL THE DICE FOR EACH BODY PART

I'm practicing...

* number concepts (quantity)
* counting in sequence
* one-to-one correspondence
* using my imagination
* creative expression
* fine motor skills

More Skill-Builders!

- **Make a whole family** of count-the-dot creatures.
- **Make up a story about your creature.** Where does it come from and what does it eat? If it has a funny number of legs, show how it would walk. How many mouths does it have? How would it eat?

Little Hands Story Corner™

The Nose Book and *The Eye Book* by Dr. Seuss

Paper-Chain Counting Calendar

Make a counting calendar so you can count how many days until your birthday, Grandma's visit, your family's trip to the beach — anything that you are looking forward to! Use this activity over and over as special events approach.

What you need

- ● Calendar
- ■ Child safety scissors
- ▲ Construction paper
- ● Marker or dark crayon
- ■ Tape

What you do

1. Use a calendar to count how many days until your special day arrives (10 days until your birthday, for example).

2. Cut two or more colors of construction paper into strips. On one strip, a grown-up can write the type of special day you've chosen. Then, you can trace over the letters with a marker.

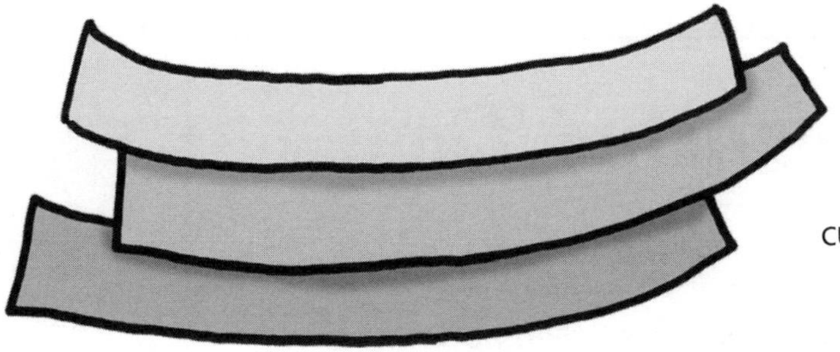

CUT PAPER STRIPS

3. Tape the ends of one strip together to form a circle. Slide the second strip through the first, and tape the ends of the second strip together. Continue adding one strip for each day until your special day. At the very end, put the strip with your special day on it.

4. Hang the chain within easy reach. Each morning, tear off one plain link and count the plain links that are left. On the morning you remove the last plain link, it will be your special day!

ADD A STRIP FOR EACH DAY

THE LAST LINK IS FOR YOUR SPECIAL DAY!

I'm practicing...

* number concepts (quantity)
* counting in sequence
* one-to-one correspondence
* fine motor skills

Little Hands Story Corner™

Ten, Nine, Eight by Molly Garrett Bang
Today Is Monday by Eric Carle
Chicken Soup with Rice by Maurice Sendak

Measuring Time

Everything we do each day takes time. A day can be divided into small or large amounts of time. Large amounts of time are called hours, and small amounts are minutes. The smallest amounts of time are called seconds.

For example, it can take a long time to paint a picture, but a very short time to count to ten.

We can use a watch to measure how long it takes to do something. It can be fun to see how long it takes you to do different things. Ask a grown-up to tell you how long it takes you to do any of the following:

- run to the front door and back
- hop all the way around the room
- count to ten
- say the ABC's
- sing a song
- put together a puzzle

There are lots of other things you can ask a grown-up to time. How long does it take you to wash and dry your hands and go sit at the table, ready for a snack? How quickly can you put away your toys after playtime?

More Skill-Builders!

- **Ask a grown-up if you can mark your special day** on a calendar in bright colors. Then, put an X on today's date. Each day, put an X on the date. To see how many more days you have to wait, just count the days between the X's and your special day!
- **Every day can be a special day,** with fun things to see, learn, and do. Decorate a small cardboard box to create your own Day-of-the Week Box. Ask a grown-up to help you cut out seven small slips of paper, one for each day of the week. Can you name the seven days?

  On each slip, draw one special thing you want to do, a place to go, or a special food you enjoy. Mix the slips of paper together, and put them in the box. Each morning, without peeking, pick out one slip of paper from the box, and find out what fun thing you can do that day!

Let's Compare

My teddy bear is big and my stuffed dog is small. They are different sizes. A car horn is loud and a whisper is soft. They are different noises. Comparing helps us to look at differences and also to notice how things are alike.

Helping Hands

Comparing and contrasting — determining what is the same and what is different — is the basis for more advanced recognition skills. Distinguishing among sounds sharpens listening skills. Visual discrimination improves observation skills, which in turn reinforces shape and letter recognition. Compare and contrast activities use memory skills while they exercise reasoning and logical thinking. They are also helpful in teaching concepts like direction, position, and size and quantity relationships.

What's That Sound?

Listen! What do you hear? There are lots of sounds all around you every day, whether you are indoors or out.

What you need

- A quiet place

What you do

1. Sit quietly for several minutes and listen carefully. Name all the different sounds you hear around you.

2. Listen again and name any new sounds that you hear. Is there a clock ticking? Is there a bird singing? Can you count all the sounds?

I'm practicing...

* listening
* sound discrimination and recognition
* vocabulary and verbal skills
* counting in sequence

Little Hands Story Corner™

Sounds All Around by Wendy Pfeffer
Polar Bear, Polar Bear, What Do You Hear? by Bill Martin Jr.
The Listening Walk by Paul Showers

More Skill-Builders!

- **Name that sound.** Close your eyes and ask a partner to make sounds with noisy things like a set of keys, a squeaky toy, or crumpling paper. Can you tell what the noise is?
- **You're a sound-machine robot!** People come to you when they want to hear different sounds. Each time they push a button on your hand, you make the sound they ask for. Can you make the sound of a bird chirping? A thunderstorm? The wind blowing?
- **Talk about how different sounds make you feel.** Some sounds make us giggle, and some sounds may even frighten us.

Mirror Pals

It's fun to stand in front of a mirror and make funny faces or stand in silly poses. Did you know you can use a partner instead of a mirror?

What you need

- Large mirror
- A partner

What you do

1. Standing in front of the mirror, balance on one foot, jump up and down, and wave your arms. Watch as your reflection does the same things you do — at the same time!

2. Now play Mirror Pals with your partner. Begin by sitting on the floor facing your partner. Decide who will be the leader. As the leader moves very slowly, the mirror pal watches very carefully and moves exactly the same way. The leader can raise an arm, make a sad face, or tap a foot. Take turns being the leader and the mirror pal.

I'm practicing...

* observation skills
* using your imagination
* taking turns
* working with a partner
* fine and gross motor skills

More Skill-Builders!

- **Try some of these motions with your mirror pal:** wiping a window, painting a picture, eating an ice-cream cone, and flying a kite.
- **Take turns acting out some everyday activities.** Carefully watch your partner's movements and facial expressions, and guess what she is pretending to do.
- **Practice Mirror Pals with the same partner.** Then, ask someone to come watch. Can he guess what you and your mirror pal are doing? See if he can tell who is the leader and who is the mirror.

Little Hands Story Corner™

In & Out, Up & Down edited by Jim Henson
Head to Toe by Eric Carle

Big-and-Little Day

Everything around us has its own size. Here are some fun ways to enjoy a special day celebrating things that are big and things that are little.

What you need

- ● Marching music
- ■ Old magazines
- ▲ Child safety scissors

What you do

1. Take a big-and-little walk. While you play the marching music, march from room to room. As you march, point to things that are big and say **"Big!"** with a big voice. Point to things that are little as you say "Little" in a very little voice.

2. Cut out pictures of big things and little things from the magazines. Make a pile of the big things and a pile of the little things. Compare all the pictures of big things with each other. Are they all about the same size, or are some bigger than others? Now try this for the little objects. Can you put all the pictures in order from the smallest object to the largest?

I'm practicing...

* observation skills
* concepts of size and size relationships
* compare and contrast skills
* fine and gross motor skills
* sorting

More Skill-Builders!

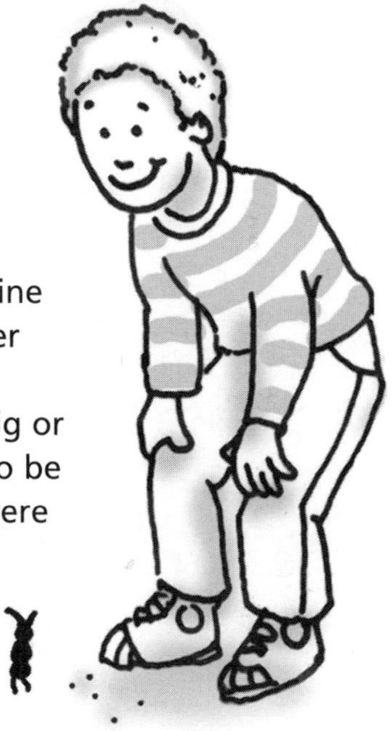

- **Look carefully at one of your baby pictures.** Then, study yourself in the mirror. Name the ways you have changed from little to big.
- **Play elephant and ant.** Imagine you're an elephant. A partner names objects and you say whether they would seem big or small to you. Now pretend to be an ant and try it. If an ant were looking at you right now, would it think you were big or little?

Little Hands Story Corner™

Big Dog, Little Dog by P. D. Eastman
It's Not Easy Being Big by Stephanie St. Pierre

Opposites Attract

Opposites are two things that are as different from each other as they can be. If you liked Mirror Pals (pages 76 to 77), you'll love playing Opposites Attract!

What you need

- A partner

What you do

Do the opposite of whatever your partner does. Watch carefully. If your partner stands up, you can sit down. If your partner smiles, you frown. Here are some more opposite actions you can do with your partner:

reach up	reach down
hop on one foot	stand still
laugh	pretend to cry
squat down	jump high
whisper	shout

I'm practicing...

* observation skills
* directional and positional concepts
* using my imagination
* taking turns
* working with a partner
* gross motor skills

More Skill-Builders!

- **Play opposite words.** For every word your partner says, you say the opposite. Here are some to get you started: hot, rainy, black, new, big, hello, tall, in, on, come, high. Take turns giving the first word.

  For a super challenge, don't say the word; instead, act it out. Your partner has to act out the opposite.

Little Hands Story Corner™

Opposites by Sandra Boynton
Exactly the Opposite by Tana Hoban
Olivia's Opposites by Ian Falconer

What's in the Bag?

You can discover a lot using your sense of touch. When you touch an ice cube, you can tell that it is cold and hard; when you pat a kitten, you can feel how soft and fluffy it is.

What you need

- ● A partner
- ■ Small, common household items: spoon, paper clip, rubber band, mitten, penny, etc.
- ▲ Paper bag

Note to adults: Small objects can present a choking hazard; please supervise toddlers closely.

What you do

1. Close your eyes and ask your partner to put an item into the paper bag.

2. Reach into the bag and describe what you feel, using words like smooth, fuzzy, rough, bumpy, hard, soft, round, straight, big, and little.

3. Now guess what is in the bag. Take a peek. How close was your guess?

4. Take turns with your partner using different items.

I'm practicing...

* visual and tactile memory skills
* sensory awareness
* vocabulary and verbal skills
* compare and contrast skills
* taking turns
* working with a partner
* fine motor skills

Alike and Different

How are a tree trunk and a piece of sandpaper alike? One way is that both are rough. Your skin and a table-top are alike, too, because they both feel smooth. Can you find five things that are rough and five that are smooth?

Little Hands Story Corner™

My Five Senses by Aliki
Is It Rough? Is It Smooth? Is It Shiny? by Tana Hoban

What's Missing?

Being a good observer means looking carefully around you. You'll be surprised at how much more you notice when you look closely!

What you need

- ● A partner
- ■ 3 to 6 common household items: comb, spoon, keys, etc.
- ▲ Small towel

What you do

1. Ask a partner to place several items on the table or floor for you to look at and touch. Close your eyes while your partner covers one item with the towel.

2. Open your eyes and take a good look. Do you know which item has been covered up? If you need a hint, feel the object through the towel or reach under and touch it. Now can you remember?

I'm practicing...

* observation skills
* visual and tactile memory skills
* sensory awareness
* taking turns
* working with a partner
* fine motor skills

Little Hands Story Corner™

The Missing Piece and *The Missing Piece Meets the Big O* by Shel Silverstein
Look, Look, Look! by Tana Hoban

More Skill-Builders!

* **Place more objects in front of you.** This time, ask your partner to remove the object rather than cover it with a towel. Now the game is even trickier!
* **Spend a minute or two looking around the room carefully.** Close your eyes and ask a friend to hide one item that's in plain view. Now, open your eyes and see if you can tell what's missing!

I'm Thinking of Something

If we ask the right questions or are given the right clues, we can figure out what someone else is thinking. Let's try it!

What you need

- A partner

What you do

1. Think of an object you can describe to your partner and picture it in your mind. For example, if you choose the word "apple," some clues to describe it are: round, red (or green or yellow), good to eat and good for you, yummy, crunchy, and grows on trees.

2. Start the game by giving your partner a clue: "I'm thinking of something that's round. Can you tell me what it is?" Your second clue might be "I'm thinking of something that's round and red." Add clues one at a time, letting your partner guess after each one.

I'm practicing...

* visual memory skills
* vocabulary and verbal skills
* taking turns
* compare and contrast skills
* working with a partner

More Skill-Builders!

- **Choose an object in the room for your partner to guess.** Your partner asks questions you can answer yes or no, like "Is it red?" or "Is it on the table?" When your partner thinks she knows what the object is, she can guess!

Little Hands Story Corner™

Can You Guess Where We're Going? by Elvira Woodruff

It Looked Like Spilt Milk by Charles G. Shaw

Touch Will Tell

Can you compare with your fingers instead of with your eyes? Try it and see!

Safety First!

Things that are very sharp, like knives or grown-up scissors, can hurt you. Other things that are very hot, like hot water or the burners on a stove, can hurt you, too. What other things can you think of that you should not touch?

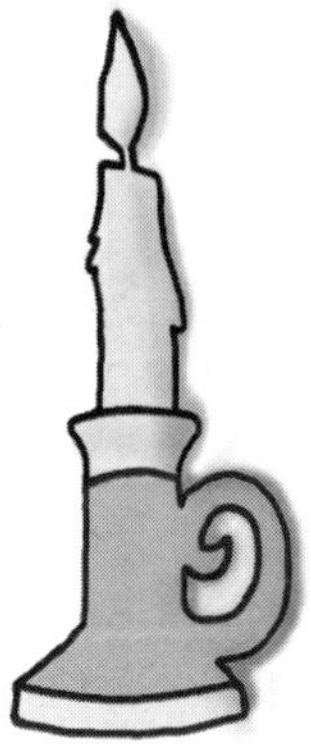

What you need

- ● Pencil
- ■ Sandpaper
- ▲ Child safety scissors
- ● Shoe box (with lid) with hole cut in one end (made by a grown-up)

What you do

1. Draw a few block letters (about 4"/10 cm high) on the sandpaper. Cut out the letters and set them aside.

2. Place the letters in the shoe box and cover with the lid.

3. Reach into the hole and pick up any letter. Feel the letter's shape with your fingers. Try to picture it in your mind. Can you tell which letter you are holding just by feeling its shape?

4. Need some practice? Try holding the letter and feeling it while you are looking at it. Then, return it to the box and touch it again.

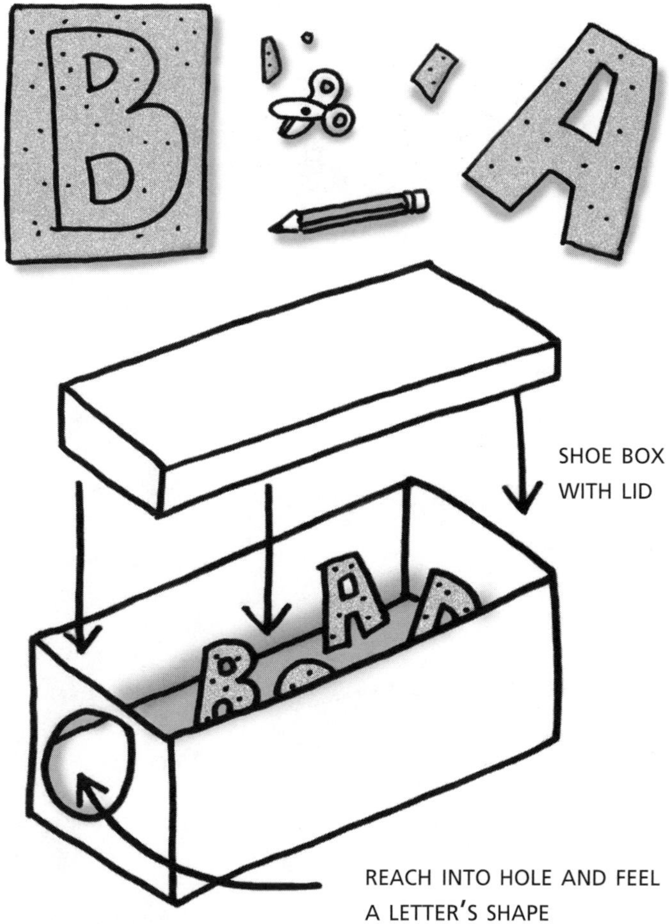

I'm practicing...

* visual and tactile memory skills
* sensory awareness
* letter recognition and formation
* fine motor skills

More Skill-Builders!

- **Try using sandpaper shapes or numbers.**
- **Close your eyes while a partner holds out from one to five fingers.** Using touch only, count how many fingers are being held up. Now count with your eyes open.

Little Hands Story Corner™

Fun with My 5 Senses by Sarah A. Williamson
Hot and Cold by Alvin Granowski

Build a Person

Eyes, noses, mouths, feet, arms, hands, and legs — we all have one or two of each of those! Use pictures to build a person the way you think these parts should go together.

What you need

- ● Old magazines
- ■ Child safety scissors
- ▲ A grown-up partner
- ● Crayons
- ■ Paper
- ▲ Glue

What you do

1. Look through the magazines for pictures of people. Instead of cutting out the whole person, cut out a hand from one picture, a foot from another, an eye, mouth, and ear from others, and so on.

2. A grown-up can draw the outline of a person on a piece of paper. Then, take turns picking a cutout part and placing it on the outline until you have built your person. How does it look?

3. Compare your person with a picture in a magazine. Do you have the same number of eyes? Ears? Hands and feet? If you want, rearrange some features on your person; then, glue your person together, drawing in anything that's missing.

Alike and **Different**

One of the most wonderful things about people is that none of us is exactly alike. Even though we share a lot of the same features, there are so many ways we are "one of a kind"!

Now look at a picture of a dog. What is *alike* about a person and a dog? What is *different*? Do people and dogs have the *same number* of eyes, ears, noses, and mouths? Can you picture a dog with a nose like yours, or yourself with a dog's ears? That would look silly! Draw your own silly critter.

I'm practicing...

- ✱ observation skills
- ✱ using my imagination
- ✱ creative expression
- ✱ compare and contrast skills
- ✱ fine motor skills

More Skill-Builders!

- **Build these other things with cutouts:** a car, an airplane, a dog, a house.

Little Hands Story Corner™

Eyes, Nose, Fingers, Toes by Judy Handley
Here Are My Hands by Bill Martin Jr.

Sort It Out!

To sort something is to put it into a group with other items that are just like it. You can sort by size, texture (how it feels), color, shape, taste, use, and more. If you put all your small toys in one bin or eat all the red jelly beans out of the bowl, then guess what? You already know how to sort!

Helping Hands

Once a child can compare for similarities and differences (Let's Compare, pages 73 to 92), he is ready for the concept of categorizing. When you help him to discover many different ways to sort and categorize the *same* items, you build flexibility into his thinking.

Gear the sorting activities to the child's level of understanding. Begin with obvious visual criteria like colors, shapes, and size. Explore the way things feel and sound to expand sensory awareness. Encourage him to use his experience, as well as his imagination, to define groups — sometimes items can be grouped together in ways that aren't obvious. Prompt him to articulate his reasoning, which will help him clarify his logic and exercise vocabulary and speaking skills.

Big and Small

Did you know that sorting is an important part of many different jobs? People sort mail in the post office every day to be sure it goes to the right houses and businesses. Grocers sort the foods on their shelves so it's easy for people to find them. You can do some sorting too!

What you need

- 5 or 6 plastic containers, varied size

What you do

1. Look carefully at the containers. Which one is the largest? Set that container on the table in front of you.

2. Keep adding one container at a time, placing each one in order of size from largest to smallest, until you've used them all.

3. Now that they're in order, try stacking the smaller ones inside the larger ones. How many can you fit into the largest container?

I'm practicing...

* observation skills
* compare and contrast skills
* sorting
* concepts of size and size relationships
* fine motor skills

Be a Music Maker!

- **Make a container drum:** Just put the lid on one container and use a spoon as your drum-stick. Drum the beat as you sing a favorite song.
- **Make container shakers:** Put a handful of buttons, dried beans, or rice in a plastic container, and put the lid on. Now shake, rattle, and roll!

Note to adults: Small objects can present a choking hazard; please supervise toddlers closely.

Little Hands Story Corner™

Is It Larger? Is It Smaller? by Tana Hoban

- **Put these items in order by size from smallest to largest:** a cracker, a banana, a rubber band, and a paper clip. What other objects can you add to make a longer row of small to large items?
- **Do you think that a small plastic container would make a good bed for a mouse?** Could it be used as a swimming pool for a baby duck? What unusual uses for plastic containers can you think of?

Toy Sort

Here's a way to have lots of fun with your toys as you practice sorting! Then you can use your sorting skills to keep your toys neat and well organized!

What you need

- Some of your favorite toys

What you do

1. Spread out the toys in front of you. Pick out the biggest toy and the smallest toy. Sort all the toys by size from big to small.
2. Sort the toys by texture — do they feel soft or hard? Make two piles, one for soft toys and one for hard toys. Which do you have more of?
3. Sort the toys by use: toys for building, toys with wheels, action figures, or stuffed animals.

Alike and Different

The pile of toys you started with are alike because they're all toys. But as you saw when you sorted them, their colors, sizes, shapes, textures, and how you play with them can be different, too. If all of your toys were exactly alike, they wouldn't be much fun to play with, would they? It's the differences that make toys — and people — interesting and fun!

I'm practicing ...

* observation skills
* compare and contrast skills
* concepts of size and size relationships
* sorting
* sensory awareness
* counting in sequence
* fine motor skills

Little Hands Story Corner™

Blue Sea by Robert Kalan

More Skill-Builders!

• **Now that you've sorted the toys, you can make some toy organizers.** Collect some large boxes. On the outside of each box, draw a picture of the kind of toys you'll be putting into that box. The next time you are ready to play with your toys, you will know just where they are!

Animal Roundup

You probably already know lots about animals. Let's use your sorting skills to see how many ways animals can be grouped by what you know about them.

What you need

- ● Old magazines
- ■ Child safety scissors
- ▲ Glue
- ● 10 index cards

What you do

1. Look through the magazines for pictures of different animals. Cut them out and glue them on the cards.

2. Now look at the pictures and make a pile of all the animals that are big. How many do you have?

3. Put all the cards together. This time, sort out the animals with four legs. Do you have any animals with two legs?

4. Try these other categories: animals that live near water; animals with feathers; and animals with fur. Did you notice that some of the same animals will fit into more than one group?

Alike and Different

What is one thing that is alike about a horse and a mouse? What is one thing that's different about those two animals? Take turns with a friend naming what is alike and what is different about some of your favorite animals.

I'm practicing...

* observation skills
* compare and contrast skills
* concepts of size and size relationships
* sorting
* counting in sequence
* fine motor skills

More Skill-Builders!

- **Look at some picture books about dinosaurs.** See if you can discover which were big and which were small, which ate meat, which were plant eaters, which had four feet, and which had only two. Can you think of some other groups to put dinosaurs in?

Little Hands Story Corner™

Flappy Waggy Wiggly by Amanda Leslie
Is Your Mama a Llama? by Deborah Guardino

Memories Box

It's a lot of fun to remember times that you really enjoyed. Make a special box to save your memories.

What you need

- ● Child safety scissors
- ■ Construction paper
- ▲ Shoe box (with lid)
- ● Tape
- ■ Crayons or markers
- ▲ Favorite things or special treasures

Note to adults: Small objects can present a choking hazard; please supervise toddlers closely.

What you do

1. Have a grown-up help you cut pieces of construction paper to cover the top and the sides of your Memories Box. Tape them onto the box. Draw pictures or designs on the box. Print your name on the top.

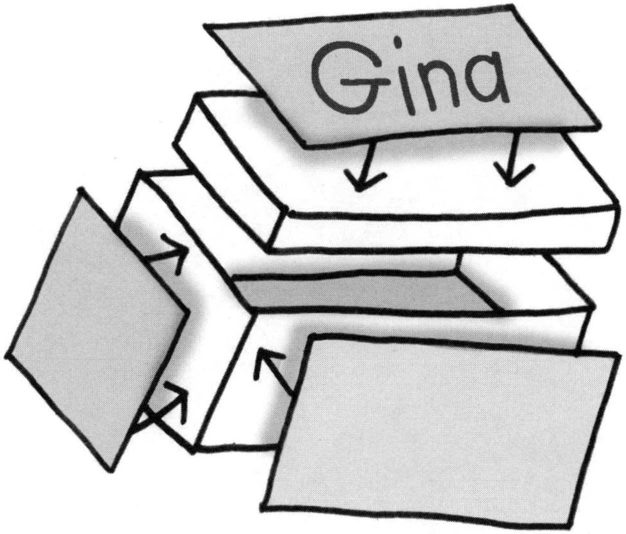

CUT PAPER TO FIT BOX SIDES; THEN TAPE ONTO BOX

2. Sort through your things to find special treasures such as favorite photographs, notes, small toys, a special stone, feather, or piece of sea glass. Put them in your Memories Box.

More Skill-Builders!

- **Share your Memories Box with a friend.** Sit and look through the box together. Show your treasures and explain why each one is special to you.
- **Have fun with photo memories.** Look at some of your baby pictures to see how much you've changed. Put them in order of youngest to oldest. Now sort them by where you were when the picture was taken (put all the beach pictures in one pile, all the photos from Grandpa's house in another, etc.).

I'm practicing...

* compare and contrast skills
* sorting
* memory skills
* creative expression
* fine motor skills

Little Hands Story Corner™

Wilfrid Gordon McDonald Partridge by Mem Fox

The Patchwork Quilt by Valerie Flournoy

Do They Match?

A beach bucket and sand go together, just as a hat, mittens, scarf, and boots belong together. Have some fun making matching groups.

What you need

- A grown-up partner

What you do

1. Ask your partner to list three or four things that belong together and one that doesn't (for example, truck, car, motorcycle, dish, bus).

2. Can you tell which item doesn't belong with the others? Why doesn't it match?

3. Try other groups. Take turns with your partner naming groups and picking out what doesn't fit.

Little Hands Story Corner™

A Pair of Socks by Stuart J. Murphy
Clifford's Neighborhood by Norman Bridwell

I'm practicing...

* listening
* compare and contrast skills
* vocabulary and verbal skills
* sorting
* memory skills
* taking turns
* working with a partner

Five-Finger Hunt

Five is a special number. It's the number of fingers you have on each hand and the number of toes you have on each foot. That makes it easy to hunt for things in this category game! You can play anywhere — at home, on a nature walk, in the grocery store, or while you're riding in the car. It will help you to see a lot more around you, too.

What you need

- A partner

What you do

1. With your partner, walk around and look for five red things. Each time you find one, count and touch a different finger on your hand, starting with your thumb. That way, you'll know when you get to five.

2. Now that you know how to play Five-Finger Hunt, choose another category of fun things to hunt for. Here are some ideas to get you started: five things that are cold, five things that are big, five things that are little, five things that are heavy, or five things that are blue. Happy hunting!

I'm practicing...

* listening
* counting in sequence
* compare and contrast skills
* vocabulary and verbal skills
* sorting
* memory skills
* taking turns
* working with a partner
* fine and gross motor skills

Little Hands Story Corner™

Old Hat, New Hat by Stan and Jan Berenstain

More Skill-Builders!

- **Want to make the game more difficult?** Look for specific objects, such as four blue cars or three dogs. The more specific, the harder it will be to spot things.

- **Play Five-Finger Hunt outdoors.** Here are some outdoor hunt ideas: five things that are green, five things that smell good, five things that have wings, five things that are four-legged, five things that are smaller than your foot, five things that live in trees.

Let's Talk About It!

The hungry dinosaur ate a snack.

I was hungry and ate a snack of dinosaur crackers.

These two sentences use a lot of the same words, but they have very different meanings, don't they? Language helps us to share our thoughts and feelings, to describe the world around us, and to enjoy all kinds of stories. Just think of all the words you know already — and every day you learn new ones!

Helping

Hands

Words — hearing and understanding, choosing and using — are of course an integral part of learning and communicating. These word-related activities increase recognition of oral and written words and sounds. They also build vocabulary, providing experiences that give meaning to the words, important for concept and language comprehension. Sharing favorite stories encourages print awareness, further reinforcing the literacy connection. These activities also provide lots of opportunity for children to practice using words as a means of personal expression to convey thoughts, opinions, and feelings.

Begin with familiar stories, nursery rhymes, and fairy tales to read aloud. Look for opportunities to focus on individual words, and reinforce their sound and meaning. Use these activities as a springboard to the world of words that kids hear spoken and see written all around them every day.

Animals in My House

Don't look now, but I think there's an elephant in your house!

What you need

- ● Old magazines
- ■ Child safety scissors
- ▲ Scrap paper
- ● Glue
- ■ Paper lunch bag
- ▲ A partner

What you do

1. Look through the magazines for pictures of animals. Cut them out and glue them onto slips of paper. Fold and place in the bag.

2. Pull a slip of paper from the bag but don't show the animal to your partner. Think about your animal — how it moves, how it rests, what it eats, and what sound it makes. Describe it to your partner. Can your partner guess what animal you picked? Now it's your turn!

I'm practicing...

* observation skills
* using my imagination
* memory skills
* taking turns
* listening
* vocabulary and verbal skills
* working with a partner
* fine motor skills

Little Hands Story Corner™

I Love Animals by Flora McDonnell
Animal Babies by Harry McNaught

More Skill-Builders!

- **Compare animals.** Both you and your partner pick a card from the bag. Compare the animals you picked, describing them to each other. How are they the same? How are they different?

Animal Races

You can be the winner every time in this race — whether you go as slow as a turtle or as fast as a horse!

What you need

- A partner
- Ribbon or rope

What you do

1. Place the ribbon on the ground for a finish line. Move far back from it, giving yourself a lot of room to move before you reach the finish line.

2. Your partner will tell you what animal you are. Pretend you are that animal as you run the race. Then let your partner take a turn. Here are some to try:

   dog — crawling on your hands and knees

   bird — flapping your wings as you "fly" forward

   ant — crawling slowly on the ground or taking tiny, tiny steps

   kangaroo — taking big, jumping steps

   monkey — pretending to swing from tree to tree

   horse — galloping as fast you can

   What others can you think of?

I'm practicing...

* listening
* using my imagination
* dramatization
* taking turns
* working with a partner
* fine and gross motor skills

More Skill-Builders!

• **Fill an imaginary zoo with animals.** Before you can add each one, you have to imitate it. Can your partner guess what each one is?

Little Hands Story Corner™

If You Hopped Like a Frog by David M. Schwartz
Funny Walks by Judy Hundley

All-About-Me Book

Create a book that's all about things you like and dislike — and it will be one of a kind, just like you!

What you need

- ● Child safety scissors
- ■ Old magazines
- ▲ Crayon or marker
- ● Construction paper
- ■ Glue
- ▲ Stapler

What you do

1. Cut out magazine pictures of things you like — and things you don't like, too. Sort them into separate piles.

2. Print "I like" or "I don't like" at the tops of several pages of construction paper (a grown-up can write them on a separate sheet for you to copy or write them lightly in pencil on the pages for you to trace over). Glue the pictures on the appropriate pieces of paper.

3. Make a cover for your book from a sheet of construction paper. Staple all the pages together. Give your book a title and draw a special picture of yourself on the cover.

4. Practice reading your book often. Remember to read the words "I like" or "I don't like" at the top of each page. As you look at the pictures, tell why you like or dislike each item.

More Skill-Builders!

- **As you think of other things you like,** add pages to your book. If you can't find the pictures in magazines, draw them yourself.
- **Discuss your book with friends.** Do they like or dislike any of the same things? What things would they add?

I'm practicing...

- ✱ letter formation
- ✱ compare and contrast skills
- ✱ sorting
- ✱ observation
- ✱ vocabulary and verbal skills
- ✱ creative expression
- ✱ language comprehension
- ✱ fine motor skills

Little Hands Story Corner™

I Feel Orange Today by Patricia Godwin
Today I Feel Silly by Jamie Leigh Curtis

Tricky Tales

It's fun to listen to your favorite stories over and over. But what if someone changed some of the words? Listen carefully for the "trick" words.

What you need

- Some of your favorite books
- A grown-up partner

What you do

1. Ask a grown-up to read one of your favorite stories aloud, changing some of the more familiar words.

2. Listen very carefully! Every time you hear a word that doesn't belong, say "Stop!" Can you tell your partner what the real word is?

I'm practicing...

* listening
* language comprehension
* memory skills
* vocabulary and verbal skills
* working with a partner

Little Hands Story Corner™

Somebody and the Three Blairs by Marilyn Tollhurst
The Three Little Wolves and the Big Bad Pig by Eugene Trivizias

More Skill-Builders!

- **Make some finger puppets** and act out your favorite story as a grown-up reads it aloud. Invite a friend to act it out with you.

- **When you hear the words "Once upon a time ...,"** what's going to happen? That's right: A story is about to begin! Make up your own "Once upon a time" story to share with your friends.

Name Noisemaker

Listen carefully for a special word and everytime you hear it, be ready to shake your noisemaker!

What you need

- ● Crayons
- ■ Paper plates
- ▲ Tape
- ● Popsicle stick
- ■ Dried beans or beads
- ▲ Stapler
- ● A favorite story
- ■ A grown-up partner

Note to adults: Small objects can present a choking hazard; please supervise toddlers closely.

What you do

1. Write your name and draw pictures on the backs of two paper plates.

2. Flip one plate over so it's right-side up. Tape a Popsicle-stick handle to the plate.

3. Pour the dried beans in the center of this plate. A grown-up can help you staple the plates together face-to-face so the beans won't fall out.

4. Choose one of your favorite stories and pick a name or rhyme that is frequently repeated in the story. As the grown-up reads the story aloud, shake your noisemaker every time you hear your word or rhyme.

TAPE POPSICLE STICK TO INSIDE OF PAPER PLATE

I'm practicing...

* listening
* language comprehension
* creative expression
* name recognition
* working with a partner
* fine motor skills

More Skill-Builders!

- **Pick a key word from another story.** This time, close your eyes as you listen. Is it easier or harder to listen for the word with your eyes closed?

Little Hands Story Corner™

Tikki Tikki Tembo by Arlene Mosel
Chrysanthemum by Kevin Henkes

Listen and Do!

Can you follow all these different challenges to make it all the way to end of the course? Sure you can, if you listen carefully.

What you need

- Open, clear play area
- Chair
- Beanbag
- 2 lengths of rope
- A grown-up partner

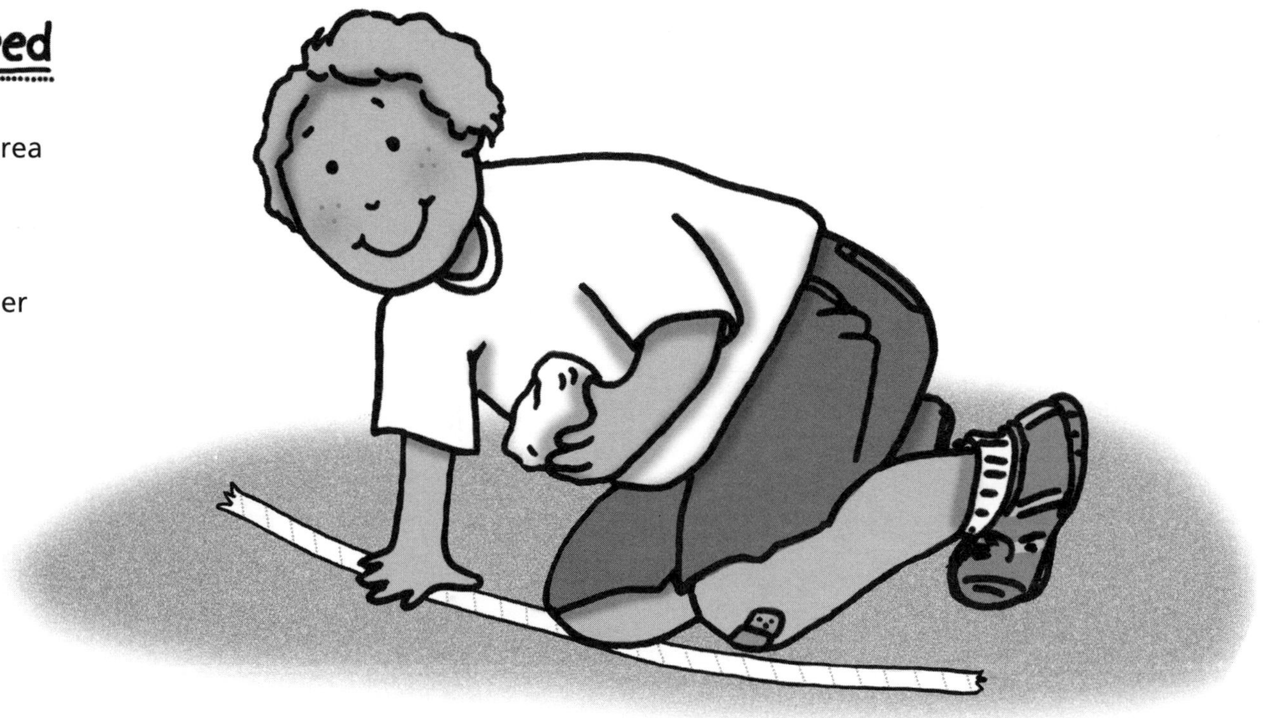

What you do

1. Set up an obstacle course using the ropes for the start and finish lines. A grown-up will call out the actions, and you complete the course. Here's an example: Jump to the chair, sit down, roll over to the beanbag on the floor, pick the beanbag up, toss it in the air and catch it, then crawl with it to the finish line.

2. Try adding different numbers of actions: jump five times to the chair, toss the beanbag in the air three times. See if you can remember the course without hearing the actions called out.

3. For added fun, ask a grown-up to time you and then practice to see if you can beat your own time!

I'm practicing...

* listening
* following sequential directions
* memory skills
* counting in sequence
* gross motor skills
* language comprehension
* directional and positional concepts
* working with a partner

More Skill-Builders!

- **Create a special Over-and-Under Obstacle Course**, such as scrambling over the seat of a chair first, then crawling under a table on the way back.
- **Set up an Around-and-Between Obstacle Course.** Walk *around* two chairs first, then hop *between* them on the way back.

Little Hands Story Corner™

Apollo by Caroline Gregoire
Over, Under & Through by Tana Hoban

Happy-Sad Masks

We all have happy days and sad days — and all the feelings in between. Words are wonderful for letting people know just how we are feeling!

What you need

- ● Mirror
- ■ 2 paper plates
- ▲ Crayons
- ● Tape
- ■ 2 Popsicle sticks
- ▲ A favorite storybook
- ● A grown-up partner

What you do

1. Look in a mirror and make a happy face. Besides having a great big smile, what else happens to your face when you're happy? How do your eyes look? On one of the paper plates, draw a happy face just like yours.

2. How is a sad face different from a happy face? One difference is that instead of a happy smile, the mouth turns downward in a frown. What other parts of your face change? Draw a sad face on the second paper plate.

3. On the back of each plate, tape a Popsicle stick to make a handle.

4. Ask a grown-up to read you a story. Listen very carefully. When the story is sad, hold up your sad mask. When the story is happy, hold up the happy mask.

Little Hands Story Corner™

What Makes Me Happy by Catherine and Laurence Anholt
My Many Colored Day by Dr. Seuss

Alike and Different

Place your two masks side by side. How are the two masks alike? Here's one way: Each mask has two eyes. Can you think of other ways the two masks are alike? How are they different?

I'm practicing...

* compare and contrast skills
* categorizing
* vocabulary and verbal skills
* listening
* language comprehension
* fine motor skills
* working with a partner

Special-Message Greeting Card

Here's a great way to send a message to a family member: a special card that you made yourself. You'll have fun creating it and they'll have fun receiving it!

What you need

- ● Old greeting cards or magazines
- ■ Child safety scissors
- ▲ Glue
- ● Crayons
- ■ Pencil

What you do

1. Look through the cards or magazines and cut out pictures you think that person would like.

2. Fold a piece of construction paper in half. Glue on the pictures. Save a spot where you can use your crayons to draw a special picture of your own.

3. Ask a grown-up to print your message in pencil on the card, so you can trace over it in crayon.

4. Print your name. Don't forget to send some hugs (O's) and kisses (X's), too!

I'm practicing...

* letter recognition and formation
* language comprehension
* creative expression
* name recognition
* fine motor skills

Little Hands Story Corner™

A Letter to Amy by Ezra Jack Keats
The Jolly Postman or *Other People's Letters* by Janet and Allan Ahlberg

Index to Early Learning Skills

Williamson's *Little Hands*® Books

To order, see page 128.

For ages 2 to 7 are 128 to 160 pages, fully illustrated, trade paper, 10 x 8, $12.95 US/$19.95 CAN.

ALL AROUND TOWN
Exploring Your Community Through Craft Fun
by Judy Press

Parent's Guide Children's Media Award
ALPHABET ART
With A to Z Animal Art & Fingerplays
by Judy Press

Parents' Choice Recommended
AT THE ZOO!
Explore the Animal World with Craft Fun
by Judy Press

AROUND-THE-WORLD ART & ACTIVITIES
Visiting the 7 Continents Through Craft Fun
by Judy Press

ARTSTARTS for Little Hands!
Fun Discoveries for 3- to 7-Year-Olds
by Judy Press

Parents' Choice Recommended
EASY ART FUN!
Do-It-Yourself Crafts for Beginning Readers
by Jill Frankel Hauser

Parents' Choice Approved
Little Hands FINGERPLAYS & ACTION SONGS
Seasonal Rhymes & Creative Play for 2- to 6-Year-Olds
by Emily Stetson and Vicky Congdon

Parents' Choice Gold Award
Children's Book-of-the-Month Club Selection
FUN WITH MY 5 SENSES
Activities to Build Learning Readiness
by Sarah A. Williamson

Parents' Guide Classic Award
Real Life Award
The Little Hands ART BOOK
Exploring Arts & Crafts with 2- to 6-Year-Olds
by Judy Press

Parents' Choice Approved
The Little Hands BIG FUN CRAFT BOOK
Creative Fun for 2- to 6-Year-Olds
by Judy Press

Parents' Choice Approved
The Little Hands NATURE BOOK
Earth, Sky, Critters & More
by Nancy Fusco Castaldo

Parents' Choice Approved
Little Hands PAPER PLATE CRAFTS
Creative Art Fun for 3- to 7-Year-Olds
by Laura Check

The Little Hands PLAYTIME! BOOK
50 Activities to Encourage Cooperation & Sharing
by Regina Curtis

MATH PLAY!
80 Ways to Count & Learn
by Diane McGowan and Mark Schrooten

American Bookseller Pick of the Lists
RAINY DAY PLAY!
Explore, Create, Discover, Pretend
by Nancy Fusco Castaldo

American Institute of Physics Science Writing Award
Early Childhood News Directors' Choice Award
SCIENCE PLAY!
Beginning Discoveries for 2- to 6-Year-Olds
by Jill Frankel Hauser

WOW! I'M READING!
Fun Activities to Make Reading Happen
by Jill Frankel Hauser